With All My
HEART

Love Unexpected

With All My HEART

Three Romantic Novellas

ANITA STANSFIELD, KRISTA LYNNE JENSEN,
SHERYL C.S. JOHNSON

Covenant Communications, Inc.

Hanging by a Moment

by Krista Lynne Jensen

IN THE VERY MIDDLE OF Montana, Kendal Johnson-Bauer stood in front of her full-length mirror, studying her new goggles and snorkel.

Her sister Lila hung up her phone. "Well, that's it," she said. "Jay can't come. Bret will be taking his place."

Kendal blinked at the mirror, then spit out the snorkel mouthpiece. "What do you mean Bret will be taking his place? Bret who?" An unsettling knot tightened in her stomach. As much as she didn't want to admit it, she knew who Bret was. She removed the goggles and added them to the duffel bag she was slowly packing.

"Jay came down with the stomach flu," Lila said. "I guess the kids have all had it over the last few weeks. I do not envy that mess." She continued folding clothes from the clean pile on the bed.

Lila was in her "mom" mode, and Kendal wondered when her little sister had become the boss. Then she remembered: twenty-three months ago this Friday, when Kendal's ex-husband had asked for a divorce, had left her and their six-year-old daughter, and Kendal's world had come undone.

"I'm sorry about Jay. So they're both staying home?" Kendal said.

Eden and Jay were old friends of Lila's, but Kendal hardly knew the couple.

"No, actually. Jay's making Eden come. After all those weeks of puking kids and laundry and no sleep, she had a hard time arguing with him. The compromise was Bret."

Bret McCray. Eden's older brother.

Lila shoved two more swimsuits into Kendal's duffel bag. "His mother was coming to take care of the kids anyway. Now she'll take care of Jay too."

"Great." Kendal took the swimsuits back out and eyed them uncertainly. Lila grabbed them and buried them in the duffel again.

"You're going to need as many suits as you own."

"I already have three in there."

Lila had taken her shopping. Summer-end clearance sales had been Lila's focus the last two months. Now, in October, Kendal had a complete tropical-vacation wardrobe, including five new swimsuits, three pairs of shorts, two sundresses she would never wear, a pair of all-terrain sandals, and her own snorkel, goggles, and fins, which made Kendal nervous with anticipation. She'd never owned snorkel equipment before.

They'd also hit the gym together, if you counted Lila cracking a whip and dragging Kendal behind her as "together." Kendal had logged seventy-six miles on the treadmill since August. She had to admit that a few weeks of exercise had made the swimsuit shopping less tortuous. And although looking good in a swimsuit was a perk, it was not the goal. She had no one to look great for except Lila's Facebook friends when the pictures posted. No. Kendal was going to be swimming, snorkeling, hiking, and helping sail a fifty-two-foot catamaran through the British Virgin Islands. Her competitive spirit had been dormant for a while, but she felt it waking up. And she would not be left behind.

"So how is that going to work?" Kendal asked. "Eden and her brother are sharing a cabin?" Kendal and Lila had a younger brother, Alan, but she couldn't imagine wanting to share a small cabin on a yacht in the British Virgin Islands with him. He'd cut her hair once while she was asleep, which was why she'd had to get permission to wear a hat for part of fifth grade. Of course, Alan was grown now and fairly cool. But she wouldn't trust him to sleep in the same room with her, scissors or no. She could probably say the same about Bret McCray.

"I'm sure they'll figure it out when we get on the boat."

"What about Jay's plane ticket? He's just going to eat it?" Kendal frowned.

Lila turned to her. "I guess. Why are you so concerned? You barely know Jay and Eden . . . But you know Bret, right? From college? You guys were like . . . buddies."

Kendal shrugged and continued packing. It was true: she barely knew Jay and Eden Kearns, but Bret McCray . . .

"I think Bret found a different flight into St. John's. He's going through Atlanta," Lila said.

Kendal, Lila and Lila's husband, Craig, their friends Angela and Dylan Rodriguez, and just Eden Kearns were connecting in Miami to go to St. John's, where they would take a ferry to the island of Tortola and crew a charter boat for seven days. And now Bret would be on board. Bret from college. Kendal scowled, pushing aside two beach towels to make room for her toiletry bag. "Eden could come by herself."

Lila placed her hand on her hip. "What is the problem? The guys need all the help they can get with the boat, and Bret has sailed before."

Kendal knew she was overreacting, and it frustrated her. It wasn't like they'd even dated. She took a deep breath. "I'm part of the sailing crew."

"I know you are, but Eden won't be able to help."

Lila had a point. Eden was petite, maybe a hundred pounds and, from what Kendal remembered, a bit on the fragile side. The heavy work of crewing and sailing a catamaran required the opposite of fragile, and Kendal had always been strong. Her mother called it *wiry*. Kendal called it "built like a plank."

"I know Eden. She's spunk personified," Lila said. "But I think the fact that she's coming at all is a big deal. She and Jay are joined at the hip. She's not one to do things alone. She's not like—" Lila paused.

Kendal gave the contents of her bag another shove and zipped it closed. "Like me." She heaved the bag over her shoulder and carried it out of the room.

But not before she heard Lila say, "I'm sorry, Kenni."

Kendal continued to the garage.

She hadn't always done things alone.

* * *

Kendal stroked the pale brown hair of the little girl snuggled into her side in the backseat of her brother-in-law's Tacoma. Craig and Lila sat up front, discussing the itinerary. They had another thirty minutes before they reached the Billings airport, and Malerie, Kendal's now eight-year-old daughter, had questions.

"How will I learn the back float?"

"I told your dad about swimming. Maybe he'll take you. It's only one week; you won't miss anything."

"I'll miss my teacher at school. Can Daddy teach me the back float?"

The girl's voice held the familiar bravado Kendal wished didn't have to exist. "Maybe. He's very busy."

"Can Cambrie?"

"I'm not sure." Kendal tried not to clench her teeth when Malerie brought up the new wife. "They take good care of you at your dad's, right?" Oh, how Kendal hated this.

"Yes."

"And you have your schoolwork to keep up. Please remember to keep your swim bag changed out. Mildew grows fast there."

"I know, Mommy. Did you know Daddy's getting a pool in his backyard? Can we move back to Florida?"

Kendal closed her eyes and kept her voice calm. "No, we can't move back to Florida. We like Montana, remember? And Grandpa's horses? And Mrs. Hill?" *Please say yes.* She could do a lot of things, but apparently, living within five states of her ex-husband and the other woman was too much. Going home to Montana had felt cowardly at first, but it was just what she'd needed. The only thing Kendal regretted was the distance between Malerie and her every June when Shane had her and on rare occasions like this. It was October, but Shane had asked to take Malerie during this vacation. It had made sense. The group's connecting flight was in Miami, and Shane had paid for Malerie's ticket.

"Yes, I like Montana too."

Kendal smiled in relief. "Me too."

To Kendal's surprise, June was all Shane had wanted in the custody agreement. He had angered her by his lack of desire to see his only child more often than that, and at the same time, the weight of a thousand anvils had been lifted off Kendal's soul. So she had to be grateful. *Grateful* didn't feel like the right word though.

"Mal, you know mean ol' Lila is forcing me to go on this trip, right? I wanted to stay home. It's a good thing you're flying with us as far as Miami because she was going to duct tape me to the luggage and throw me in the back of the airplane."

Lila turned from the passenger seat, shock on her face. Her husband, Craig, chuckled. Kendal could always count on him to get the humor lost on her sister.

"No, she wasn't, Mom." Malerie giggled.

"How do you know?"

"Because Lila is smaller than you, and you would break through the duct tape and go all ninja on her."

"I would?" Kendal winked at Lila, who finally smiled.

Malerie nodded, humor in her gray eyes. She executed a karate chop in the air. "Hi-*ya*! And besides, you want to go on this trip."

"How do you know?"

"Because on your Google search history, it's all 'British Virgin Islands' and 'snorkeling' and 'sailing a pontoon yacht' and 'sharks in the British Caribbean' and stuff. You're excited."

"You check my search history?" Kendal's mind raced to make sure she didn't have anything to feel panicked over.

No. Her search history would be quite tame—and before searching began for this trip, probably really boring.

She leaned over and kissed the top of her daughter's head, smelling strawberry shampoo and mint gum. "Clever girl. I love you."

"I love you too." Malerie looked up at her and smiled.

* * *

Pulling her carry-on in one hand and holding Malerie's hand in the other, Kendal took a deep breath and stepped off the exit ramp and into the Miami International Airport. She could already feel the familiar humidity in the air, though the air conditioners were running on full, even in October. Their group gathered near the flight postings and shed their jackets and sweaters.

She heard Shane's voice above the crowd.

"That's right, it's probably freezing in Montana."

Kendal turned, and Malerie shouted, "Daddy!" She ran to him, and he swung her around. As her daughter and ex greeted each other, Kendal couldn't help searching for signs of her replacement.

Grow up, Kendal. The woman has a name.

Still, she was relieved to see no sign of the new Mrs. Bauer. *Thank you for that, Shane.*

Shane's hand sat on Malerie's shoulder as he waited for the rundown. He'd grown a mustache. Kendal couldn't fathom why.

Here we go. Kendal stepped forward. "Okay, she's just gotten over a sinus infection and only has two days left on her antibiotics. You wouldn't even guess she was sick, but she has to finish them. Two times a day. And she's got a loose tooth."

"See?" Malerie demonstrated by wiggling it for her dad.

"Wow, any day now," he said.

Malerie nodded.

"She's horrified about missing a whole week of swim lessons, so it's important to her that she keep up while she's here." Kendal continued. "Don't forget sunblock. Also, she's having a hard time with division, and she's got the awful times tests they do, so if you could make sure you—or whoever—signs those off, that would be great. She just has one suitcase, the pink one, and Lamby and Dangles are in her carry-on. Please make sure they don't get left behind anywhere; you know what happens if they do. And I know I'll be in an international calling area"—*Oh, please, not the tears, not now*—"but if Mal needs to call me for *anything*, please have her—"

"Kenni," he said.

She looked up. "What?"

"We'll be okay. Don't worry."

Kendal blinked. Something had changed. "But I'm going to worry."

He laughed and nodded. "I know. But try not to. If we need to contact you, we will."

She frowned. Where was the bristling manner, the biting remarks to camouflage his guilt?

"Thanks for letting me have her. You look great. Have fun," he said.

She blinked again.

The others had kept a respectful distance, but now Lila was at her side. "Hello, Shane. Nice 'stache. You lose a bet?" Her tone had not been spiteful enough to make Malerie suspect her aunt's true feelings, but Kendal covered a smile. Lila turned. "Kenni, we need to make our connection."

Kendal nodded. She opened her arms to Malerie, who flew into them.

"Can you call me lots?" Malerie asked.

"No, honey, not lots, but I will every chance I get. You mind your dad, okay? And watch out for gators."

"And you watch out for sharks."

"Deal." Kendal squeezed Malerie tight, kissed her, and let her go.

Malerie and Shane both waved. Kendal waved back, swallowing hard.

"Bye, Miss Mal!" Lila called. She turned, pulling Kendal in the opposite direction. "That went well, didn't it? He had sense enough not to bring the Camry."

"Cambrie."

"Whatever."

"I guess." Kendal looked behind her. Shane and Malerie were gone.

"Malerie seemed okay," Lila said.

They caught up to the others, who were already on the move.

Kendal swiped at a tear. "Yep. She's a trooper." She halted and looked behind her again. A man ducked around her at her sudden stop, and Lila turned, looking confused.

Kendal threw her arms out. "Actually, I have no idea how she is. She's eight." She sniffled loudly. "And she loves her dad, and I'm not sure what just happened, but what if he wants her for more than just June?"

Lila reached back and took her hand. "What are you talking about? She's doing great, Kenni. And lots of parents leave their kids to get away for a long-overdue vacation now and then. Just because Shane was decent for once doesn't mean he's looking to split the year with you."

Kendal nodded. She knew parents got away. Lila and Craig had left their boys with Craig's parents in Helena. And it wasn't just Shane who'd agreed to the custody arrangement. Cambrie certainly hadn't pushed for more time with her new stepdaughter.

Eight days. That's all. Eight days until Malerie was back in her arms. Much better than a month. Much better than an entire summer.

She changed the subject as they resumed their hurried march. "So how much do you think a swimming pool would cost?"

"Where are you going to put a swimming pool?"

Kendal glanced behind her again. "Montana."

* * *

Kendal emerged from the crowded women's bathroom of the St. John's airport arrival terminal feeling refreshed in clean shorts and a tank. She'd changed in one of the narrowest bathroom stalls ever designed, had banged her elbow, and had nearly dropped her sunblock in the toilet, but as the cool air of an electric fan hit her skin, she knew it was worth it. She located her group, who had gathered near one of the luggage conveyers.

She studied her travel companions. The trip had been Angela and Dylan's idea. They'd done this with another group last year, same charter company and itinerary, but this time had invited their friends Eden and Jay (the no-show), and Lila and Craig, who had in turn invited Kendal. Another couple from the East Coast who had been part of Angela and Dylan's first trip would join them later at the boat. The man had a captain's license and would be heading the crew, which consisted of all the men and Kendal, because she had sailing experience and was the only woman interested.

So, four couples and Kendal. No, scratch that. Three couples, Eden and Bret, and Kendal, and five cabins on a fifty-two-foot catamaran yacht. She didn't know whether to embrace her fifth-wheel status or cringe because of it.

Lila turned, saw Kendal approaching, and smiled. Big. She thumbed toward a figure in a ball cap pulling a huge duffel off the conveyor. He reached again for some kind of bulky equipment wrapped in a tarp and duct tape. His T-shirt fit him well. Really well. Nice tan. Nice . . . but it wasn't like Lila to check out guys at an airport.

Kendal raised her eyebrows at Lila in question, but when the guy settled his luggage and tugged off his ball cap, revealing short, dark blond waves, Kendal knew why Lila was smiling like a kid in line at a carnival.

Bret McCray had arrived in St. John's. And he was looking right at Kendal.

He grinned. He could still pull off that reddish scruff of facial hair. Dang. "Hello, Magic."

Oh, good. College nicknames. She smiled. "Hello, Bret."

Eden grabbed her arm. "Kendal, I think it's crazy that you know my brother."

"I agree," Kendal said. "But then, most of the girls on campus questioned their sanity after knowing your brother."

Eden laughed, and Bret put his cap back on his head, pulling the bill low, but Kendal could still see the grin.

"Aw, that's not fair," he said. "*You* never really knew me, did you?" He locked eyes with her from under his cap.

Kendal couldn't read his thoughts, and she was having trouble reading her own. She wanted to ask, *How do you know someone who doesn't want to be known?* But she was tired, and they had seven days to share on a boat, and she had absolutely no desire to paddle up that river of yesterday, so she conceded with a shrug.

He watched her a second longer, then, seemingly satisfied, turned and grabbed his stuff, and the others followed suit. Kendal grabbed her own duffel and wondered how feasible it was to stay on the opposite side of the boat from Bret McCray at all times.

No, that was too dramatic. After everything she'd been through the last couple of years, her past—if you could even call it that—with him was a mere blip. She glanced over at him talking animatedly to Angela and Dylan. So she went to college with Bret. Okay. And now she was on a trip of a lifetime with good, adventurous people. And time. Time for herself, as Lila had put it. And she hadn't had that in a very long while.

The flights had been long, she'd just seen Shane again, and she'd left Malerie behind. She pulled in a deep breath and vowed to be better.

She followed the group out of the arrival area and into the sunshine of St. John's Island. Low green hills stretched before her, and palms reached up to blue sky in scattered groups everywhere, supported by giant mounds of hot pink and orange azaleas. The white buildings of a university pocked the emerald slope in front of them, and Kendal wondered what it would be like to attend college in a tropical paradise. Not much like Missoula, she concluded. She looked around. Far less snow.

After some negotiating, Dylan waved them all to follow one of the eager cab drivers to a small black SUV with enough room to store their luggage, including Bret's big duct-tape job, and themselves. Kendal squeezed in next to Lila and Craig in the center seat, and they were off to the ferry port.

Angela and Eden chatted behind them while Dylan and Bret leaned forward in the front seat and peppered the driver with questions about the island. The driver answered their questions in his thick island accent, and as Kendal listened, she watched a different world pass by the windows. So much color. Poverty, wealth, commerce, tourism, all packed together in the humid tropics. Bicycles, motorbikes, limousines, rusty old trucks, taxis, and flowers everywhere flowers could grow. They passed a schoolyard filled with cocoa-skinned children dressed in white shirts and black shorts, running crazily after a soccer ball.

She found herself leaning forward, nose almost touching the window, taking it all in.

"First time here, Magic?"

Kendal pulled away from the window and faced Bret, who had turned in his seat, his arm draped over the back. Nobody had called her Magic in a really long time, and she wasn't sure she liked how it made her feel. She shook her head. "You?"

"No. I tend to lean toward Mexico."

"Often?"

He shrugged. "Once or twice."

She nodded, wondering if he meant once or twice a year or simply once or twice ever. What had he been doing with himself during the last . . . twelve years?

Oh heavens, had it been that long?

"Have you been?"

She looked at him. "Where?"

"To Mexico?"

She took a deep breath and concentrated on what looked to be a resort and the ocean beyond. "Yes."

"What part?"

She shook her head. She didn't want to remember what part and why she'd gone to Mexico or how much she'd loved it and wanted to go back. But she hadn't gone back. "Merida."

"Merida, huh? Unusual."

She nodded. The colonial city was not on any coast, not like Cancun or Puerto Vallarta. Not the usual first choice when vacationing in Mexico. Which is why, another lifetime ago, she and Shane had chosen it for their honeymoon.

Bret went on. "But Merida is beautiful. The square at night—quite a party. Some incredible ruins in that area." He paused, and she knew he was waiting for her to ask a question in return, to tell him she'd seen Chichen Itza and Uxmal, or that she'd eaten guanabana ice cream off the Plaza Grande, or to ask him what parts of Mexico he'd been to or when he had visited Merida.

Dylan interrupted her nonanswer. "There's the ferry port." He turned back to everyone with a grin. "Who likes ginger ale?"

* * *

"The ferry schedule is posted . . . but they don't keep to it?" Kendal asked, plopping herself down on a wooden chair in a pub on the second level of the ferry house. They'd checked their luggage . . . into a pile on the ferry dock, and it and they would wait for the next ferry to arrive. Meanwhile, they ordered lunch.

"You're on island time now. I'm pretty sure the posted schedule is for looks." Dylan winked and pushed a frosted mug filled with a golden, gritty-looking liquid toward her. "This, however, is mandatory."

"This is ginger ale?"

"Yup. They make their own right here. Grows hair on your chest. Ginger ale back home is for lightweights. After this, you'll never go back. It's very sad, actually."

She sniffed it, and her nose tingled. "What's in it?"

"Some fizzy stuff, pineapple juice, honey, and gobs of ginger."

Lila sipped hers first. "Mmm." She sipped again. She gave Kendal a thumbs-up.

Kendal lifted her glass and thought a moment. "Here's to . . . island time."

"To island time." They all raised a glass.

The sweetness hit the tip of her tongue, the bubbles farther back as she swallowed, and then the spice of the ginger hit her in the nose. Her eyes watered. "Whoo." She looked down at the amber swill. "I can't believe there's no alcohol in this."

"Crazy stuff," Dylan said.

A waiter delivered their food, and Bret took out his camera. Not a compact auto-flash snap camera but a big, cumbersome telephoto-lens instrument of photography.

"Still taking pictures, huh?" Kendal asked as she picked up half of her grilled mahimahi sandwich.

"You bet," he answered, and he snapped a picture of her midbite.

"Oh, that's lovely," she said through her mouthful.

"Beautiful," he said, looking at the screen on the camera.

She paused, jolted by his candor. She felt the warmth of a blush come on.

"No worries," he continued. "I just got the sandwich. Looks like you ordered well."

Craig chuckled, and Kendal hated that her blush only deepened. She elbowed Craig in the ribs.

"Here," Lila said, pulling her own little camera out of her bag. "All of you lean in and smile."

Kendal knew the command was for her. She managed a smile, grateful for the distraction.

The sandwich was delicious. She *had* ordered well.

* * *

The ferry boat slammed into another wave, and Kendal began rethinking the sandwich.

"They don't call it the Tortola Fast Ferry for nothing," Angela shouted from the seat in front of Kendal.

The weather had turned while they'd eaten in the pub. They'd heard a rumor of a tropical storm brushing past the islands, but nobody had seemed certain of how close it would come. Rumor or not, the waves en route to Tortola were tall and angry, and the ferry didn't care.

"It's like a roller coaster ride," Dylan shouted, smiling as the boat rose again. It slammed down hard and nearly threw Kendal from her seat.

"I don't. Like. Roller coasters." Eden looked a little green.

Kendal reached into the side pocket of her bag and pulled out a roll of Dramamine. She held it out to Eden across the aisle. "Have you taken any yet?"

Eden shook her head. Dylan had warned them to take a Dramamine every morning of the trip until they could tolerate the rocking. But this wasn't rocking. It was . . . upheaval. Eden took the pills and popped one in her mouth. Just as she lifted her water bottle, the boat rose higher than it ever had, and Kendal was sure they'd gotten air. A moan of anticipation filled the cabin, and as the boat crashed back to the water's surface, several passengers screamed.

Eden spilled water down the front of her.

"Are you okay?" Kendal asked.

Eden nodded. "Yeah. Refreshing. I got the Dramamine down anyway." She leaned forward and rested her forehead on the seat back in front of her.

"It should kick in soon. We'll be to Tortola in just a few minutes."

"'Cause it's the fast ferry." Eden groaned.

Kendal laughed. "Right."

She caught Bret watching her over his sister's back.

"You like this," he said.

"Are you crazy?" she answered. But as the boat slammed down again, she couldn't help the laugh that was knocked out of her.

"See?" Bret said.

She shook her head. "It's the best. Let's just rent one of these for the week."

Eden groaned.

The door from the bridge swung open, and the man who had been introduced as the owner of the vessel staggered out with a drink in his hand. Kendal guessed it was not ginger ale.

"Rum and coke, maybe?" Bret asked as though reading her mind. He winked at her.

The man walked along the aisle with a wide smile, assuring his passengers not to fear; it was just "a little tossy," and all eyes seemed to be focused on whether or not he would spill his drink, which sloshed dangerously in the clear plastic cup. He informed them with a slight slur that they would need to fill out their "entry to a foreign country" forms and that it would be best to have them filled out before they docked in Tortola and went through customs. They'd left the American Virgin Islands behind, and the British Virgin Islands were somewhere beyond this raging tempest.

On cue, little duplicate forms made their way up from the back, and the man turned to leave just as another blast of the waves knocked the boat forward. Down he went to his knees, and everyone gasped.

"Not to worry," he shouted from the floor. He lifted the glass high. "Didn't spill a drop."

* * *

"The name on your passport is different from the name on the form." The statement came out as a question in thick islander.

"No, it's the same, see? K-E-N-D—that's an *A*, that's an *L*. The boat ride was choppy so it was hard to write."

"No, this name . . . Bauer, on your passport. Eanan on the form."

"Eanan? No, that's Bauer. See? Like I said, the boat ride." Kendal made big wave movements with her arm as though the customs officer was deaf and needed some form of sign language to get the point across. He watched her dully. She stopped.

The second customs officer leaned over and said something to him about checking against a driver's license. Kendal pulled hers out and gave it to the officer. He sighed, nodded, and waved her through.

For the first time, she considered dropping her used-to-be-married name. Nobody mixed up Johnson.

"Ladies and gentleman," she heard the customs officer call behind her, "make sure your forms are legible. Make sure your *u*'s don't look like *n*'s and such."

People in line got out their pens and started marking over their forms.

She rolled her eyes and turned back to get her waiting luggage and found Dylan, Craig, and Bret making giant wave motions with their arms. "It was the boat ride," they said in unison.

She walked past them to the shuttle. "I'm on vacation with third graders."

"Oh, c'mon, Eanan. That was sixth grade at the least," Bret said.

The shuttle took them around to the opposite side of the bay, to Soper's Hole, which mainly consisted of a grocery store, a restaurant, some tourist shops, and the charter company, all painted in sherbet colors. Out in the bay, the rental boats gleamed white and shiny.

"We can't take the boat out today. They're afraid the storm may get too close." Dylan sat down on one of the benches outside the charter office, plainly disgruntled.

"So . . . what does that mean?" Angela asked.

"It means we can get settled on the boat, stay here tonight, and hope-fully head out tomorrow. If you girls want to get some food shopping done now, maybe just for breakfast in the morning in case the storm hits closer and we're stuck, the guys will get everyone's luggage on and divvy up rooms."

In the small but clean market, the girls bought some yogurt and bananas, a jar of mango jelly and some bread, and chocolate. They made a quest of finding bottled ginger ale like the one in the pub and bought a few different kinds to try. By the time the women returned to the dock, the guys were ready with a dinghy.

Bret stood at the front of the "raft with a motor" and gave a hand to anyone who wanted it.

"Magic," he said with a nod of his head as she stepped into the boat. She wobbled but stayed upright. "Kendal."

"Like a Kendal in the wind," he sang.

"Oh, please," she said to nobody in particular. "Make him stop."

He chuckled, and she sat down near the motor end of the boat.

She read the name of the yacht as they approached: *Wild Thing.*

Sounded like a spring-break party vessel. She renamed it in her head. *Midlife Crisis Thing.* No, that would be her ex-husband's boat. How about *Cut-Me-a-Break Thing?* Perfect.

The dinghy lurched as they pulled up to the boarding deck. Eden squeaked, and Angela kept her from falling forward.

"Ladies, welcome aboard." Craig reached for each of their hands as they made the small leap to the deck. "Get used to this; it's our only way on and off the boat for the next week."

The vessel was impressive: clean white and neat, the interior decorated simply, with orange and navy-blue cushions and painted wedges of fan coral anchored to the narrow shelf encircling the main salon, which had a big galley, a bar, and a dining table and banquette seating for everyone.

Dylan approached Kendal, looking somber. "We need to talk," he said and motioned for her to follow him as the other women oohed and ahhed about the quarters.

"What's the problem?" She couldn't imagine why he'd have an issue that involved her this early into the trip. She may have been a little grumpy, but she'd behaved.

"So you know how the floor plan on the website had a smaller cabin and we figured it would be perfect for you, being single?"

She nodded and continued to follow him out of the main cabin and around to the side of the boat. She grabbed a rail to keep her balance. "Right. No problem."

"Well, I'm worried you might have a problem."

They were on the bow of the boat now, which had several hatches scattered over the top of it.

She looked at him expectantly.

"This is not what I expected for your quarters, but this is your bunk." He leaned over one of the hatches, pulled it up, and let it flop open to the deck.

She peeked over. Straight down was a bed. Nothing more. Two molded steps jutted out of the near wall and led down to nothing but a crisp white blanket and sheets atop a full-size mattress that filled the space against every wall. A small hole in one side looked like it served as a closet. Or a small animal den.

"But I thought this was connected to the main room." The floor plan on the charter company's website showed a small bunk with what looked like a doorway from the dining area.

"I thought so too, but we must have misunderstood. There's no air conditioning in this bunk, so they've installed that." He pointed to a tiny fan screwed into a corner. "You'd have to prop the hatch open. It's the only way in or out."

She steadied herself as the boat rocked, and she looked to the southwest. The storm was far off, but dark rain clouds loomed in the distance. Even the water in the bay seemed to be darkening.

She thought a moment and took a breath. She wasn't going to let this dampen her "me time." It would be secluded. And small. She stopped wringing her hands. "Okay. Awesome. I'm fine with it. Except if it rains. I mean a little rain, fine. But if the only way in or out is through this hatch, and if the storm hits and I need to run from here—" She looked toward the back of the boat and the entry to the main cabin. She shuddered. "Not that I'd need to run, but . . ."

Bret appeared out of nowhere and peered over the open hatch. "I'll take it."

Kendal shook her head. "No, really, you don't have to do that."

"Why not?" He looked at her, his hazel eyes searching hers. Challenging her.

"Because this is what I agreed to—"

He stopped her. "Listen, I'm the last-minute tagalong here. You think I want to share a bunk with my sister? She's great and all, but . . ."

"But I'm fi—"

"Nope. I call it. You can take my spot with Eden. Have you seen the cabins?"

She shook her head.

Bret rolled his eyes at Dylan, then turned back to her. "Look, you go check out the cabin and then come tell me no. Besides, I know something you seemed to have forgotten."

She frowned at him.

"Three words. *Claus. Tro. Phobia.* Or have you forgotten the elevator incident?"

She pressed her lips together. Lila was probably the only other person on this boat besides Bret who would know of her fear. She worked through it most of the time, could hide it. She remembered the elevator incident. Someone had called the fire department. And somebody's therapist to talk her down. But that kind of reaction was rare. She looked back at the hole in the deck.

He leaned toward her. "Let me take it."

She forced herself to look away, to Dylan, who looked at her as if to ask why this was a difficult decision.

She looked back at Bret. "Okay. I'll trade. But if a storm comes—"

"I'll head inside, sleep on the couch. No worries."

She nodded and breathed out the nagging fear she'd suppressed since the moment she'd seen the bunk. "Thanks."

He grinned at her. "Not a problem."

She shook her head and smiled back.

"Go on. Go check out that luxury suite of yours. I need to move into my *pad*."

She rolled her eyes but made her way back to the main cabin. Everyone seemed to be settling in, so she explored as she looked for Eden.

A set of steep stairs on each side of the boat led to cabins below, which branched off a main hallway running fore and aft. Lila waved at her from a fore cabin, and Kendal noticed that Angela and Dylan seemed to have the biggest room. No surprise, since they'd done all the groundwork for the trip. A small hallway bathroom was situated between those two rooms, though each had their own bathroom en suite. This would have been her bathroom, but now it was Bret's. She made her way back up to the other side of the boat. She descended those stairs, gripping the handrail, and passed an empty cabin. Then she found Eden and her own luggage already waiting for her.

"Hello," Eden said and motioned her in. "You don't mind, do you?"

"No. Thanks."

"I thought that first closet could be yours, and we have a few drawers to split up."

She arranged a hanging toiletry organizer in the bathroom and latched the door open so it wouldn't slam shut on her. "You can just shove your empty luggage in the bottom of the closet."

Kendal dragged her duffel over. "So you knew I'd be staying with you?"

She shrugged. "Bret knew about the situation with your *room*. He insisted. To be honest, I don't mind at all. He snores."

"So do I."

She paused and looked at Kendal wide-eyed. "Oh . . . that's okay—"

"I'm kidding." She smiled. "At least I think I'm kidding. I hope I'm kidding."

Eden laughed with relief and shook her head. "I don't care. Really. It's a good trade." She sat down and held her stomach.

"You feeling any better?"

She nodded. "Some."

"I'm sorry your husband got sick."

"Yeah, me too. I'm less scared of stuff when he's around. Less nervous about silly things."

Kendal continued to unpack, wondering if she'd been less scared of stuff when she was with Shane. No, she concluded. Not really. If anything, she'd been harder on herself with Shane. More nervous.

"Do you want the outside of the bed? Bret told me about the claustrophobia."

Kendal paused and looked at Eden. "He did?"

Eden nodded.

"Yeah, thanks."

*　*　*

Joe and Beverly Bastion were a surprise. Kendal had figured Angela and Dylan's East Coast friends would be more . . . youthful. Closer to the rest of the group's age.

Joe's silver hair and cruise shorts, Hawaiian shirt, and captain's hat had Kendal smiling.

"Don't worry," he said as he shook her hand during introductions. "I only wear it on the boat."

"That's only because I said something." Beverly smiled. "At least he got rid of the knee socks." She placed her hand to the side of her mouth.

"Last year." She took Kendal's hand. "Kendal, what a pretty name. Like a candle in the wind. Like that Elton John song."

Kendal laughed under her breath and glanced sideways at Bret. He was talking to Joe and hadn't heard. "Yeah, kind of like that. It's nice to meet you."

And it was. Beverly, or Bev, as she insisted everyone call her, soon took her place as activities director, party planner, and general mother hen to all of "you beautiful young people." The Bastions moved into their cabin and met everyone else above for the walk-through orientation with the charter company owner, whose Australian accent was so thick Kendal had a hard time understanding him. As they moved to the mechanics of sailing the yacht, Kendal stayed with the guys while the other girls went to change out of their travel clothes.

As the men followed the Aussie above, Joe turned to her. "Are you going to help us out here?"

Her defenses rose, but she smiled. "Yes, if that's all right." She felt Bret's attention turned their way. "I used to own a little sailboat." A big sailboat, actually.

"In Montana?"

She smiled. "No. I lived in Florida for nine years. But there are places to sail in Montana."

"Ah. Well, terrific. You have your captain's license?"

She nodded.

"Well, I'll be. Glad to have you on board, Cap'n Kendal."

She watched her feet on the deck and grasped the side railing. "Oh, please don't call me that."

"First Mate?"

"Just Kendal."

His eyes crinkled with his smile. "As you wish. Now pay attention. One of us has to know what we're doing."

She returned the smile, and her defenses faded. As Joe moved on, she glanced up and caught Bret's look of approval.

"What are you looking at?" she asked.

He shook his head. "Nothing. You think you know somebody, that's all."

"You think you know me?" She chuckled at the idea.

Bret shrugged. "Maybe."

"Let me help you out. You don't." She moved past him. "And I don't know you."

* * *

Bret McCray only half listened to the Aussie. He didn't look at Kendal again, but that's exactly where his mind was.

Why the attitude? He'd remembered her claustrophobia, had even given up his cabin for her. He'd only been surprised that she had a captain's license. He really shouldn't have been. She'd always been the kind of person to just go for it. But in his mind, she'd also been in Montana this whole time, and people generally didn't acquire a sea captain's license in that state.

But she'd married a guy . . . a banker? From Florida. And until his sister had mentioned Kendal's name and this trip, that's all he'd heard of her. He'd looked forward to seeing her again. But she had a point. What did he really know about her?

He remembered her laughing. She liked to laugh. Her smile was great. Guys liked her. She was one of those women guys were comfortable with. Bret and Kendal had flirted. Played basketball and volleyball on intramural teams and weekend tournaments. Her competitive drive had challenged him. She had a powerful spike. He'd been on the receiving end of that maneuver many times, often to lose the point.

And there was Rick. His roommate. Who'd been crazy about her.

He shifted his body weight uncomfortably and folded his arms.

Aw crap.

Now he remembered.

* * *

They grabbed dinner at Pusser's in Soper's Hole. Coconut shrimp and jerked chicken. Rice and beans. Conversation was light, fun. They'd decided being stranded on a boat in Soper's Bay, Tortola, in the middle of the Caribbean, was better than being stranded, well, anywhere else.

But Kendal noticed Bret's subdued mood. His head was often down, his smile strained. She couldn't help but feel a twinge of guilt for that. She'd been short with him. Sheesh, she'd practically told him to get lost.

But his sister, Eden, smiled and laughed with the others.

Kendal noticed the color back in Eden's face. "The Dramamine worked?"

Eden nodded in gratitude as she pulled a cheesy bite from her quesadilla. She chewed and swallowed. "Take one every morning, right?"

"Yup, before you even feel queasy. In a couple days, you'll be more comfortable on that boat than on land."

Eden looked doubtful but grinned. Kendal wondered how old she was. If she hadn't known Eden had three kids and had gone to school with Lila, she would have guessed fifteen. Sixteen. And she'd been through something. Leukemia? Something as a child. And she'd beaten it. So she might look like Kendal could block her out of the key and send her sprawling with a bump of her hip, but Eden had strength in that petite facade. And Kendal liked her.

After dinner, they headed back to the yacht. The water rocked under the dinghy, and Joe pointed to jumping fish in the dark: silvery flips catching the headlight and skimming alongside the boat. The group didn't say much, full of food, tired after the long flights, quieted by the spectacular sunset at the restaurant. Clouds had been crowding against one another like ships in a boatyard, and the setting sun had made good use of color, light, and vapor. But it was dark now. Kendal looked across the dinghy to catch Bret's gaze. He didn't look away quickly, but he did look away.

She looked down at her coral toenails. Lila had insisted they get pedicures for the trip. Pedicures were not Kendal's thing.

She remembered the time she and Bret and Rick had gone rock climbing at Mill Creek Canyon. Bret hadn't bothered to get a date. Rick was above, his movements raining down crumbly pebbles on her head and into her handholds. She'd slipped. Bret, below, had caught her. He'd just caught her. Reached out his arm and pulled her in. He hadn't needed to. They were all harnessed and clipped. But he had, their faces inches from each other, startled like they'd never pressed against each other on the court, sweating or breathing hard.

Kendal swallowed, her face warm, and she welcomed the cool breeze lifting off the water now. She'd caught herself smiling.

* * *

Eden snored.

The rain hit hard at about two in the morning, and Kendal lay awake just as the sound of the generator quit. She sat up, grabbed her phone for a light, and left the cabin. The twin pontoons would keep the boat steadier than her old single-hulled cruiser, but it still rocked in a storm. She could hear the pelting roar washing over the windows and deck. She climbed up the stairs as the boat swayed, and just as she reached for the sliding door leading outside, it slid violently open, and there stood Bret's silhouette, dripping wet, shirtless, and cursing under his breath because he was as startled as she was.

"Where do you think you're going?" he asked in a hushed, urgent tone. Lightning crashed behind him, and she blinked as the sky lit up.

"The generators quit. No air, no water pressure, no fresh water, no electricity."

Lightning crashed again, and a wave of rain threw itself at Bret's back. He motioned behind him. "Plenty of that out here."

For a moment, her mind blanked as the rain dripped off Bret's chin and ran down his shoulders.

A smile began at the corner of his mouth. "In or out?" he asked.

Kendal blinked again and shook her head. *Nice, Kendal.* "Out." She threw her phone into a utility drawer next to the sliding door and traded it for a Maglite. She pushed past him under the covered outdoor dining area and over the textured deck surface to the hatch concealing the generators. He followed her, and they both lifted the hatch to observe the now-silent piece of machinery.

"It's a good thing we're not out to sea in this," he said.

She nodded. Then looked up. "You were in the hold." She referred to the little bunk that would have been hers.

He nodded and shrugged, shedding drops of rainwater as he reached for a tool bag down next to the generator. "Where else would I be?"

She paused. Then she reached for the generators' power switch, flipping it off and on with no response. "Thanks again—Whoa." The boat rocked, and since she'd been leaning into the hatch, she lost her balance and slipped forward.

Immediately, Bret grabbed her, wrapped his arm around her middle, and pulled her up to him, bracing against the hatch frame with his other hand. Her back pressed against his chest, her soaked T-shirt the only thing between them. "Careful there," he said into her ear.

She couldn't respond right away, as her adrenaline seemed to turn her brain to mush. But as the boat settled again, she found her voice. "I'm fine now, thanks," she said and pulled away from him. He let her go, and she refocused on the generator.

He produced a screwdriver and handed it to her, taking the Maglite and holding it so she could open the panel. "No problem."

After a few minutes, they had one of the generators running again.

"Great job," he said. "We may be able to get some sleep tonight."

"You might. Eden snores," she answered.

He smiled. "I know."

* * *

Kendal woke to the sound of a baby's cries. Eden was gone. Confusion and a bit of panic gripped her in her drowsiness, and that instinct to protect and comfort that had brought to life when Malerie was born kicked in. She frowned and pulled herself up, peering through a now-open porthole. Who would have a baby out in the bay?

The anger of the storm had dissipated. The one generator they'd been able to restart during the night hummed low in the belly of the boat. But she heard the baby cry again and searched through the porthole, sure it sounded like it was just off the side rail. Her eyes were drawn to the lush green hillside along the edge of the bay, a mile from her porthole.

Then she saw them.

A small herd of brown goats dotted the green slope, now a mess of wind-torn shrubs and trees. Their bleats carried clearly across the calm water.

She felt both relief and foolishness at her alarm. Goats could take care of themselves. They moved along, foraging. She could pick out the specific cries now. A couple of smaller goats trying to traverse over fallen trunks. Her gaze roamed the hillside, to the dwelling built farther up the steep hill. A boy sat perched with a stick, watching the herd. A man she assumed was the boy's father worked at making piles of the litter, clearing a path toward the goats.

She lay back down and sighed, listening to the soft bleating and the lapping of waves. She had no idea what time it was, but as she allowed the odd sensation she'd awoken to fade, new noises took over: men's voices in discussion, someone taking a shower, the water pump laboring. She smelled toast and coffee.

A knock at the door preceded a soft "Hello?" Eden peeked around the door, and when she saw Kendal's eyes open, she smiled and entered with a small plate.

"I made you some toast and jam. You picked out the mango jelly, right? And there's coffee up top, but I didn't know how you liked it."

Kendal sat up and ran her hands through her tangled hair. She'd fallen into bed wet and exhausted. But at least the starboard side had cool air all night and warm water and flushing toilets for the morning. The charter company would have to do the rest of the repairs. Bret had collapsed on the banquette as he was.

She took the toast, now famished. Through her bite, she asked, "How did portside do last night?"

"Oh. Portside. That's the left, right?"

"Right."

"Right?"

"Port is the left side. You were correct."

"Right. They did okay. Just flung off the sheets. We're sharing the showers on this side. Bret said you were amazing."

"He said that, huh?"

Eden nodded, smiling.

Kendal swallowed her last bit of toast. "Are they going to get the other generator fixed?"

Eden sat down on the end of their bed. "They're at it right now. We have the clear to head out as soon as everything passes inspection. A few of us were going to take the dinghy over to Peter Island and snorkel while they finish up. Do you want to come?"

Kendal smiled. "Yes."

She had certified in scuba. Shane had seen to it. She hadn't minded the beginning courses in a large, clear chlorine pool, and then she'd endured being enclosed in the cold depths of bay water, the deep dark pressing in on her claustrophobia. But she'd certified and had accompanied Shane on several excursions, mostly fighting panic, with Shane assuring her each time that it just took practice. She'd wanted to believe him. She'd wanted to believe him about a lot of things.

Snorkeling had been about the same. Though no courses or certifications were necessary, Kendal still had a difficult time fighting the hovering panic that set in whenever Shane got too far away, the current became too strong, or the water turned too dark. And because Shane thought snorkeling was the baser, more mundane water exploration, their few holiday excursions included rental equipment, and she somehow always ended up with leaky goggles and loose fins because of her too-big-for-a-woman, too-small-for-a-man size feet and, in her panic, ended up swallowing more saltwater than what she blew out of the snorkel.

Maybe this was why she loved up-top water adventure. The challenge of sailing did not bring the panic. And she was perfectly contented to captain a boat, dive into the water on occasion, and swim on the surface.

But now she had her own snorkel equipment. She'd bought it herself. An auto-valve snorkel and the perfect fins and a mask she had tested in the bathtub. No leaks. Her decision. The underwater sea life of the islands had promised to be spectacular, and if they happened to spot a sea turtle and Kendal couldn't report back to Mal that she'd swum alongside it, she wasn't sure she could live with herself.

Her only hesitation was the fear of being left alone. And it proved to be a silly fear. The group stayed together in the clear turquoise water like a long-legged school of fish, making sure to point out the different corals and tetras. Everything worked. Kendal's anxiety disappeared, and even when she took the opportunity to explore alone for a bit, the panic never came. She smiled.

And then she saw it.

She surfaced from her practice dive and blew out her mouthpiece. "Guys! Hey, guys, a sea turtle!" She saw bobbing heads turn, and she didn't wait. She dove back under and carefully approached the large turtle meandering along the sandy bottom beneath her. She felt a hand on her arm and turned to see Bret. He gave her thumbs-up, and the turtle rose from the bottom. Bret motioned to Angela, who held an underwater camera. Kendal swam around to the other side of the turtle as it continued to gracefully rise from the bottom, and Angela took the picture.

She'd done it. Kendal grinned around her mouthpiece, and after she surfaced again, she laughed.

* * *

The sails were out and full. Bret cranked the capstan while Dylan pulled the halyard into a fast-falling pile, keeping it out of the way and in its place, all the while following directional shouts from Joe at the wheel, who also directed Craig and Kendal on the other side. Finally, Joe was satisfied, they tied the knots, and the wind carried them swiftly over the water toward the Bitter End and dinner.

Bret gazed up at the white sails, taut and pulling. He climbed onto the upper deck and leaned back, where he caught a glimpse of Kendal on the starboard side. Her white cottony shirt blew this way and that against her body, and she too watched the sails, a look of triumph on her glistening face.

That look of triumph—that's what he remembered. And her laugh as she'd surfaced from their swim with the turtle. She'd been giddy. And everything had come back to him. Their games and competitions, their trash talk and high fives. She was a grueling opponent, but when they teamed up, they were nearly impossible to beat. They enjoyed it. Reveled in it. And that, for the most part, had been their relationship.

Until his roommate and friend, Rick, had seen in her what Bret had missed. While Bret was off flirting with anything in heels, Rick had asked Kendal out. Then he'd asked her out again. And then Kendal and Rick were the team.

Bret had brushed it off. She wasn't his type anyway. It was the competition, the rivalry, her athleticism he appreciated.

Until he'd kissed her. Right there against that hard rock wall, with Rick clueless, scrambling up above, raining silt and pebbles down on them. Bret had grabbed her in her fall, pulling him to her in an instant of sheer panic as if she was really falling, and then with the realization that she was okay and so close, he'd kissed her hard, and she'd returned it with more passion than he'd ever imagined. He remembered surprise and pleasure and heated recklessness. And her softness. Rick didn't even know she'd slipped, and he'd kept yammering on about the treacherous rock face as he climbed. Finally, she'd shoved Bret away and, without another word, had resumed climbing, fast, to catch up with Rick.

It was all he could do to regain his composure, call up an insult to Rick's impatient taunts, and when they all had reached the top, he and Kendal couldn't even look at each other. Out of breath, heart pounding, he told himself it was from the climb. Rick was Bret's friend. The guy was crazy about Kendal.

And Bret was kicking himself. Even later, when she had coaxed a look from him, a question, a plea in her eyes, he had turned away. He'd thrown himself at the next bouncy blonde whose name he couldn't remember, and their games had stopped.

He watched Kendal again from the other side of the sail. She was more sarcastic, short-tempered, suspicious. Life could do that to people.

But then she'd laughed.

* * *

They'd tied onto a mooring ball off Bitter End and spent a leisurely afternoon exploring the marina village, the boardwalk shops, and the bakery. Dylan and Bret spoke to some guides about kitesurfing conditions, and before dinner, the group found a sandy beach, laid out in the sun, read, and slept in swaying hammocks under palm trees. Bret dragged his tarp-duffel into the dinghy, and he and Dylan spent a couple of hours kitesurfing.

Kendal pretended to read but couldn't take her eyes off the guys fighting the waves, the wind, getting that sail up and skimming over the water like flying fish. Something about the challenge of it stirred her. She'd always loved the dare—the test, to see how far she could push her body. It had been a long time since she'd taken on any real push though. The scuba, of course, and maybe her rise to a challenge was the reason she allowed Shane to press her there. She'd begun running again with Lila. But after considering for a moment, the biggest challenge she'd taken on for a long time was her pregnancy and giving birth to Malerie. She'd done all she could to do that right, and her body had responded as promised in the books she'd read. As Malerie grew, Kendal had wanted to do it again. But Shane was hesitant. "Not now. Maybe in another year. It's good to space them out."

Now that she thought about it, what did he know? She'd been the caregiver, the present parent, the decision-maker when it had come to their daughter. He'd been a good dad but only when it suited his schedule, his ideas, his available emotion and energy.

On the other hand, if they'd had another child, it would have been one more spirit to crush in the divorce.

She shook her head. *It's past. It's done.* They'd both learned things about their relationship, and she didn't want to revisit it. She just wanted to make sure she didn't repeat mistakes.

Kendal watched Bret lean back against the pull of the sail.

Whatever had or hadn't happened between them over a decade ago was not a mistake or even a challenge. It just was. And she had to admit, the memories she had of Bret weren't entirely unpleasant. Most of them were fun. More than fun—they were epic. She'd been too hard on him.

She leaned back against her lounge chair and tried to focus on her book.

The pub where they ate dinner boasted a fine foosball table, and after they'd filled themselves on local sandwiches and drinks, a number of people in the group threw out challenges, and Kendal found herself in a foosball tournament to the death. The table somehow survived the onslaught, and after she spun her kicker and made the winning goal against her brother-in-law, who cried out in pain, threw his arms in the air, stumbled backward into the wall, and slid down in slow, dramatic defeat, she turned to find Bret waiting. This was it—the championship match. He steadily placed his hands on the knobs, stared her down with a cool, calm gaze, and said, "Show me what you've got."

She narrowed her eyes back at him. "I think you've seen what I've got." The corner of her mouth lifted as the crowd around them "oohed."

He remained steady. "Something tells me you've been holding back."

She leaned forward. "You couldn't handle it all at once."

The crowd snickered and yelped.

But he leaned forward too. "Watch me."

Kendal swallowed.

His brow lifted ever so slightly, and Angela dropped the ball onto the playing field.

* * *

Kendal lay on her back, her hands behind her head as she watched the black sky above her veiled in miles upon miles of stars. Bret appeared out of the dark and sat next to her. He handed her a blanket, and she took it.

"Thanks. Don't get too comfortable."

He chuckled. He'd beaten her, thoroughly, for the championship. Beautifully. She was still recovering.

Back on the yacht, they'd gathered on the large trampolines stretched between the forward pontoons. Primarily used for sunbathing during the day or for enjoying the cool spray of the ocean as they sailed, they became the perfect stargazing spot at night. The perfect place to think. Or not think at all. It had been a long time since Kendal had enjoyed not thinking anything at all.

"Is Eden okay?" she asked. Eden had not quite shaken the motion sickness for the day and had barely eaten her dinner.

"She's in bed. She took another Dramamine. I think she'll sleep."

She nodded and placed the blanket behind her head. The night had cooled, but she wasn't ready to be covered up. The sea air embodied everything she loved about this place—the scents, the warmth, the taste—and she wanted it to embrace her as long as she could allow. She hadn't shivered yet.

"That was fun," he offered.

She nodded in the dark. She couldn't deny that.

"You were always fun," he said.

She turned and looked at him. Time was such a strange thing. People separated. They aged. They wrinkled, gained weight, lost hair. She studied his eyes in the dark. The eyes didn't change though. No matter the time or distance, people could recognize each other there. Could see their younger selves in an old friend's eyes.

"What have you been doing, Bret?"

He smiled and leaned back on his elbows. He took a minute, probably deciding where to begin.

"I'm in Bozeman. Officially, I'm a CPA. But I run a guide service. Fly fishing, kayaking, whitewater rafting. Seasonal. I have a house on my parent's Appaloosa ranch, and they remind me every day of my responsibilities to the family business. But that's okay. I have an ex-wife in Butte." He paused, and his brow furrowed just a little. "And two boys who I miss more than anything."

She watched him sharing who he'd become. "What are their names?"

"Colt—he's seven, and Cannon, who's five."

Her chest tightened in empathy. She didn't ask what happened. She didn't care to know what had caused the divorce just yet. But she knew the hurt of missing your child as though a part of your heart was misplaced and living with knowing you might have done something different to prevent its loss.

She smiled. "Good boys?"

He nodded. "Terrors."

She laughed.

"I get them every other weekend. That's how I live my life. For two and a half days every two weeks."

She said nothing, and they watched the stars for a few minutes.

Finally, he asked what she knew he would. "And you?"

She kept her eyes on the sky.

"I have a little girl. She's eight. The divorce was a year and half ago. She and I rent a little house in Lila's neighborhood in Great Falls, and I work the front desk at Optimum cable. She loves my dad's horses, Hello Kitty, and swimming. She's everything."

She took a deep breath. "Her father only gets her one month a year. But I think he wants more now." She turned and looked at Bret. He watched her back.

They said nothing in the moments that passed, but she allowed herself to learn something from him in the silence and carefully tucked it away.

Gradually, Bret turned and called out across the trampolines. "Where to tomorrow, Captain Joe?"

"The Baths, young Mr. McCray."

Bret smiled at Kendal and chuckled.

"The Baths," they both said in unison.

* * *

In researching the trip, Kendal had learned that on the Virgin Gorda island, there lay a playground. Rocks and boulders seemed to have been arranged by a giant child who'd stacked them just so to create a world for his little action figures—caves, tunnels, wave chutes, splashes of light, dark corners flickering, ladders, platforms, knotted ropes, even grip holds were cut into soaring, smooth monoliths in angles and curves, inviting visitors to explore, to venture, to make good of what the child had done for them.

To take pictures.

"Smile."

Kendal turned her head and obeyed as two cameras snapped. Lila nodded at her image screen. "Good one, Kenni."

"Perfect," Bret said, slinging his pro camera more securely around his shoulders. "The lighting here is incredible."

"Let's go, kiddies." Dylan rubbed his hands together. "We'll make it to the top for a late lunch."

They climbed and crawled, waded and hid. The trail took them low and high, and occasionally they left it. Kendal couldn't help attempting to scale a perfect wall above a shallow blue pool. Her muscles strained to make the necessary holds, but she remembered what to do.

"Careful, you might slip," Bret said as he passed beneath her, moving on to another cave.

"Wouldn't want that to happen," she replied.

He turned and snapped another picture of her, then checked the image. "Beautiful," he said.

She chuckled and reached for another hold. "What, the rock?" she muttered.

"Nope."

She turned back to him. He looked at her a second longer and then turned to follow another tunnel. She watched him for a moment, then finished the short climb and sat on top of the boulder, catching her breath.

"Hey."

Kendal turned sharply at the greeting. Eden stood just behind her, hands on hips, grinning beneath her huge sunglasses. Kendal recognized that mischievous smile. Just like Bret's.

"How did you get up here?" she asked.

"There's a rope ladder on the other side." Eden peeked over the edge. "You climbed this side?"

Kendal nodded, feeling a mixture of pride and foolishness. "I think I took the hard way."

"You're Spiderwoman." She sat down next to Kendal.

"Only when presented with a wall." She looked Eden over. "You feeling better?"

"I am. Finally slept like a log, and here we are on terra firma, and this is a fascinating place. Look." She pointed to a hole in another rock above them, which was obviously inhabited by a family of birds. Next to it, another hole displayed a small but balanced stack of smooth white stones. "Somebody climbs higher than you."

Kendal laughed. "Very possible."

"I wish Jay could see this. He'd be scrambling all over." She sighed.

"Have you talked to him?"

Eden nodded. "He's a little better. Feels like he's been hit by a truck. I talked to the kids. The washing machine broke, and it sounds like my mother is ready for her own vacation." She sighed. "I'm going to be paying for this in mom-guilt for a while."

Kendal smiled. "Ah, mom-guilt. The driving force of daughters everywhere. I hope it's worth it for you."

Eden looked around, out past the rocks to the turquoise ocean, and lifted her face to the sun. "I'm determined to make it so. Have you called your little girl?"

Kendal nodded. "This morning, really quick. They were headed for the zoo."

"Sounds fun."

"Yeah . . ." Kendal had been surprised and thankful and jealous to hear about the trip.

Eden stood and motioned Kendal to follow. "C'mon. Bret says there's a little tree with thick leaves like rubber. You can carve your name on a leaf, and it stays, like a tattoo. I want to leave my name on this place."

Kendal followed her down the rope ladder. "That's allowed?"

"I guess. It's just on the one tree. I hear it's kind of pretty." She hopped down to the ground.

Kendal landed behind her. "You and Bret are close?"

"Um, we weren't really growing up. I was so much younger. He was done with high school before I even got there. But, yeah, since the divorce. He really turned to his family then." She hopped down to the sand and waited for Kendal. "Three years ago and horrible as, well, you know, right? And thank goodness he came to us and we were there. He's a great guy, you know? He deserves to be happy."

Kendal nodded.

Eden leaned her head to the side. "I hope you don't mind me saying so, but you guys have great chemistry."

Kendal balked. "What? Who?"

Eden shrugged. "You and Bret. I've just noticed, that's all. I'm good at that. Ask Lila."

"Lila?"

"Yup. I played matchmaker there, remember?" She laughed. "Like I had to do much. Those two were dripping with chemistry. Bret and his ex on the other hand—"

They both turned their heads at a sharp whistle. Bret stood a ways off at the top of another rope ladder, hands on his hips. Why did he have to be so aggravating and appealing at the same time?

He motioned for them to follow. "The others have moved on and up. Tall drinks and fresh water await us, ladies."

Eden answered. "But we want to play some more."

Kendal nodded, recovering from Eden's earlier observation. "Eden says we need to vandalize a tree or something. Is that legal?"

He switched directions, motioning for them to follow. He shook his head. "There's one in every family," he muttered.

At the tree, Kendal held Bret's pocket knife over the thick, emerald-green leaf she'd chosen. Other rubbery leaves on the squatty tree bore initials, dates, *PE+SM4ever*. Gold scarring laced the plant from every angle. Kendal wasn't usually one to vandalize property, especially a living thing.

"You're sure this is okay?"

He held his hand out to the line of people waiting behind them.

She took a deep breath as Bret waited. Eden had already moved on, shouting that she'd beat them to the top. "Have you decided?" he asked.

She nodded. Kendal cut into the leaf. M-y M-a-l-e-r-i-e.

She handed Bret back his knife, and he smiled. "Perfect. Feel better?"

She nodded. "I'll tell her I left her name on a tropical island. Are you going to write something?"

He paused, then reached behind her, brushing her arm, and lifted a leaf.

She read it, and her cheeks became warm. "Magic."

She looked at him. He shrugged.

"My favorite basketball player."

She nodded, and he turned to go.

He'd been the one to give her that nickname after their first scrimmage: "Kendal Johnson, guard. Tight with the pass, drives for the score. Just like Magic."

They made their way up the trail, Bret stopping to take a few more pictures. "Do you still play basketball?" he asked.

She laughed. "No."

"Volleyball?"

"No."

"Why not?"

The question caught her off guard. She hadn't played for years. "I guess I don't know anyone who plays." She heard the lameness of the excuse in her voice. She knew there was a volleyball league at the rec center, but she wasn't a member, and she didn't know anyone on the teams. Everything was her job and Mal's school and keeping it all afloat.

"You were good. You should find a team."

She smiled at his simplification. "I'll look into it."

"You should."

"I said okay."

He paused and looked at her. "Good."

"Good." Sheesh. What did he care?

They passed more cliff walls. "You still climb?" he asked.

He kept his focus forward. She wondered if he was remembering that day in Mill Creek. The thought made her pulse pick up. "Not as much as I'd like."

He turned and raised his brow.

Why'd she say that? Would he read into that more than she'd intended? As if rock climbing was a metaphor for . . . kissing with passionate abandon? Oh no, was it? Carefully, she added, "My dad still likes to go. We've gone to Hellgate a couple times since I moved back." To clear her head, her dad had said, force her to focus on something other than the hurt and betrayal.

Bret nodded. "Have you gone out to the Smith River Valley? Some excellent climbing there."

"No, I haven't."

"You should try it sometime. Only a couple hours from Great Falls. You can soak in the hot springs after."

"Sounds great."

"It is," he said.

"Good." What was with him?

"We should go sometime."

She paused, but he kept walking.

He said no more about climbing. "Have you heard anything of Rick?"

"Rick?" She resumed walking. "Rick Stanton? Wow, um, no. Why?"

"Just curious. He's in Virginia. Works in Washington."

She nodded. She'd known Rick would end up in Washington. That was the dream. "Is he happy?"

Bret stopped. She waited.

"Did I say something wrong?"

"No, I just had to consider the question. I think he's happy. Great wife. Three kids. He beat cancer last year, so yeah . . ."

"Oh no."

"Yeah. Happy he beat the cancer. Definitely." He continued walking.

She pressed her hand to her stomach. "I feel horrible."

"Why? Because you dumped a guy, broke his heart, and then he got cancer?"

She knew he was teasing her. She could see the lift at the corner of his mouth. She deserved it. It was exactly how she'd sounded.

"No. I just feel terrible for anyone who has to go through that. He was a sweet guy."

He turned to her. "He still is. And a good friend. The kind you'd never want to betray or upset." He watched her. "Or hurt by stealing his college girlfriend. Even when . . ."

She stared. She needed to say something, she knew that, but he'd somehow just confessed in the most nonmaddening way that the one spontaneous kiss they'd shared a very long time ago had actually happened, and out of loyalty to his friend, he'd been unable to act on it. And he'd sort of just asked her to go rock climbing.

Too much time passed, and he looked away.

"Okay," she blurted out.

He quickly looked back at her. His brow lifted. "Okay?"

She nodded "Yeah, okay." She continued up the stone path bordered by tropical trees, past him, and she heard him follow, but then she stopped again and turned.

"Even when what?" she asked.

"What?"

"You said you wouldn't steal his college girlfriend, even when . . ."

He pulled his faded cap a little lower and looked up at her. He took another step closer, and she warily stood her ground. Her heartbeat picked up a bit, and she was suddenly sorry she'd asked the question.

He met her gaze. "I wouldn't steal his college girlfriend, even when I knew she might want to be stolen."

He moved past her, the grin returning to his face.

She fought a smile. But then she frowned.

"Hey," she called after him. "Why does that make me feel guilty again?"

He continued up the path. "You're a brazen hussy."

She stopped and picked up a fallen fruit and threw it at his back. He turned, looking shocked, and scooped up a handful of fruit and pits. She turned away as they hailed down on her.

"Oh, now you're in trouble." She bolted up the stone steps rising out of the path, grabbing his hat off his head as she passed him.

"Hey, my hat!"

"Not anymore."

They raced up the path, and she managed to keep his hat just out of reach as he attempted to catch hold of her or trip her up. She escaped each time and continued up, her laughter drawing the attention of those around them. Just as she reached the top, he grabbed her and pinned her against the old stone wall.

Out of breath, he held her tight. "I win," he said, his voice rough, his smile triumphant.

She shook her head, her heart racing from the contest. "I still have the hat."

He glanced down at the ball cap smashed between them, still in her hand. "A technicality." He watched her, catching his breath.

"You have to let go of me to get it," she said.

His brow furrowed. The sun glinted off his dark blond waves. "What if I don't want to?"

Her gaze jerked back to his. If he loosened his grip, she'd bolt again with the hat. Wouldn't she?

She swallowed. "You look better without it."

"Do I?"

She nodded. "I'd be doing you a favor tossing it over the wall."

Slowly, he loosened his grip around her. He still kept ahold of her waist, pulled close to his, but he rested a palm against the rock wall behind them, never taking his eyes off her. He had debris in his hair. Her heart still pounded, but it wasn't so much from the run.

He leaned a bit closer. Defeat hovered close, but she didn't seem to feel much fight. Then he said, "My boys gave me that hat."

Darn. He'd played the ace card.

"Well," she said, swallowing, "I guess you win." She moved a bit, but he still held her against the rock. Why was it always a wall with him?

His gaze had intensified.

She peeked up at him. "You have nutshells in your hair."

He didn't blink. "So do you."

"What does that say about us?"

The corner of his mouth lifted. She hadn't played like this in so long. And never with Shane. And suddenly she felt fear. Fear of what could be. Fear of having it. Fear of losing it again. This was just flirting. Competition. Just as it had always been with Bret.

But he didn't look like he was thinking about losing.

She looked around at the wall behind her. "This seems to be a thing with you," she said. "Do you practice this technique or does it come—" Her eyes widened, and she squirmed hard. "Huge spider! *Huge spider.*"

He let go immediately with a shout and twisted away, eyeing the place on the wall she'd focused on. "Where? *Where?*"

She shook out the ball cap as he danced a bit, and then she placed it on her head. She turned and walked away toward the entrance to the restaurant and swimming pool. "I must have been wrong." She swayed her hips a bit in victory. "I win," she sang.

"Cheater," he called after her.

She smiled.

A voice called from above. "I told you."

Kendal looked up and found Eden perched on the stone wall, watching.

"Chemistry. Dripping."

Kendal ignored the comment. "Get down from there and come swim with me."

* * *

The following morning, the *Wild Thing* sailed on toward one of the favorite spots on the tour. Sandy Cay, a small island just off the tip of Sandy Spit at the eastern edge of Jost Van Dyke, had been donated to the public as a natural preserve by some Rockefeller or other. Surrounded by fine white sands, clear blue waters, and only a few mooring balls, it was the perfect place to relax, hike, swim, sunbathe, and imagine you had an entire deserted island to yourself. After the excitement, crowds, and activity of the Baths, Kendal looked forward to this being a different kind of paradise.

As the island drew near on the horizon, the sunbathers on deck gathered to watch the approach.

"What is that?" Eden pointed to an object floating in the water just starboard.

"Looks like a cupboard door."

"And that?" Eden pointed again.

This object was white and puffy. Dylan grabbed a grappling hook from its place, and as the object neared, he snagged it and brought it closer.

"It's a pillow."

Craig had jumped down by the swim ladder to grab the wooden object. "It's a hatch door."

"Is that a yogurt cup?"

Kendal watched the cup of blueberry yogurt float by, followed by a sheet of sticker labels: *Bed Sheets, Towels, Blankets, Life Jackets.* She looked in the direction the debris was coming from. Joe had already done the same and was on the radio.

"*Big Digs*, this is *Wild Thing*, come in."

Kendal searched the area. To portside about sixty yards off was another yacht. *Big Digs.*

"*Wild Thing*, this is *Big Digs*, copy."

"Hello, *Big Digs*. We're coming up on a lot of debris in the water. Anything we need to know? Over."

Then Kendal saw it. Up ahead, still, small, and white in the shallows between Sandy Spit and Sandy Cay was another yacht. A single spout of water shot from its aft deck, and a smaller, older boat floated nearby.

Bret emerged with binoculars.

The radio talk continued.

"From what we know, nobody's hurt, but it's sinking fast. The tugboat's trying to get her off the shallows before she sinks too deep. Brand-new boat. First run."

Joe clucked his tongue. "Shame. Any details on what happened?"

Kendal could see what happened. Even from here, the color of the turquoise sea between the spit and the cay never deepened. Technical gauges and depth finders would hardly be necessary to warn a captain not to take a boat through that narrows. Whether it was sand or coral or rock, it was a huge risk to attempt running a boat through and made no sense to try since the cay was small, a third of a mile wide, and easy to navigate around to get to the other side.

"We heard the owner put his rig on autopilot back at Camanoe. Set his course and then fell asleep."

Joe swore.

"Woke up and scrambled to pull it out, but . . ."

"Too late."

"Yup, too late."

Kendal moved to the front of the trampolines and leaned against the cable railing. Other boats were gathering, keeping their distance but watching intently. Two more pumps had been placed on the boat's deck, and they had moved close enough now that Kendal could see a couple of men climbing around like ants, their dinghy bobbing on a rope attached to the dying boat. Longer, taut cables connected to an old tugboat attempting to pull the yacht out of the shallows and into deeper water. She could hear its engines now running loud and hard. But from what Kendal could see, it wasn't making much progress.

"What a waste." Lila drew up beside Kendal.

"Yes."

Lila took pictures as Bret passed around his binoculars. Joe spoke on the radio as more info trickled in.

The pumps, five now, spouted water off the yacht like the Bellagio fountains, and the boat hadn't moved much except to sink deeper into the water, into the sands. But the tugboat kept pulling. The current brought them more and more bits and pieces of the wreck.

"Are you okay?" Lila asked.

Kendal blinked and turned to her sister. She unclenched her fists from around the cable and swiped quickly at an escaped tear. "Yeah."

But she wasn't. Something had torn at her. Sickened her. "I think I'll go below for a while."

"Okay." Lila's look of concern asked more questions, but she remained silent.

"Come get me when we're balled at the cay."

"Okay." Kendal turned but felt her sister's hand on her arm. She turned back.

Lila only offered her a smile. That smile. The one that said, "I don't know exactly what you need, but I'm here."

Kendal squeezed her sister's hand and made her way below, as confused by her emotional reaction to the wreck as her sister had been.

* * *

Sandy Cay simmered in the midday sun. Kendal followed behind as the hike took them under shady treed canopies breaking out into blue sky and rocky shoreline and up through low, green brush and cactus jutting upward like little skyscrapers above Central Park. They reached the top of a black rockslide and climbed down to the other shoreline, where giant waves broke violently against large boulders. Obsidian-black and pearl-white rocks the size of fists and worn smooth clattered against one another as the waves crashed and receded.

Wet with spray, Kendal wanted to shout above the noise, to send rocks crashing against the stone walls. She didn't know what she'd shout. Or what good it would do. *Curse that sinking yacht. Blast that little tugboat.* A cry for psychiatric evaluation? Instead, she pushed herself back up the rockslide, not stopping until she reached the top.

Back on the main trail, dozens of hermit crabs crossed in front of them and mounds of brain coral rose up from beneath the spongy ground. Lizards raced over rotting leaves, and large red crabs tucked themselves farther into splayed tree roots.

During it all, Kendal became more and more frustrated. She hardly said a word and trailed behind. And her frustrations with herself grew because they were on a bona fide rustic Caribbean island so alive with natural beauty and sweltering romance that if they happened upon a pirate and his wench entangled in an embrace, they could think nothing of it. "Of course!" they would shout. "Arrr!" And the other couples would follow suit. Sheesh, Angela and Dylan had already disappeared.

And there she stood in a grove of trees, feeling insignificant and sick, staring up at an ancient mahogany glowing from the backlight of the island sun.

"Almost reverent, huh?"

She looked at Bret. The expression on her face must have surprised him because he immediately showed remorse for bothering her.

"Are you all right?"

She looked back up at the tree and nodded. "Tired, maybe."

"I think the trail ends back at the beach here pretty soon. Do you need some water?" He held out his water bottle.

She showed him hers. "Thanks."

"This is an incredible place."

She agreed. It was a place she'd run away to, if she could run away.

"Are you sure you're okay?"

She allowed a smile. "Just lots on my mind."

That was true. Something about the wreck in all this paradise had dropped an anchor in her momentary peace. It had jolted her back to reality and the foreboding she felt concerning Malerie and their life in Montana and the divorce and Shane and his new life.

"C'mon." Bret shouldered his camera and nodded toward the trail. "I know what you need."

She raised an eyebrow at his confidence, but he was already walking away so she followed. He looked back on occasion to make sure she was still there, but he didn't press for anything more.

Finally, they reached a large granite cube, the Rockefeller's monument on the island that marked the beginning and end of the looping trail. Bret removed his camera kit and set it carefully aside on some fallen palm leaves, then reached for one of several fallen coconuts scattered around this part of the island.

He handed the raw, husky thing to Kendal.

"What am I supposed to do with this?" She looked around. "I seem to have left my machete on the boat."

He laughed and grabbed another coconut for himself. He shook it, listening to the liquid sloshing inside, and then lifted the fruit high and smacked it down hard on the edge of the granite monument.

Kendal gasped. "Can you do that?"

"Apparently so." He inspected the damage to the coconut. Then he looked up at her. "And I'm winning."

She looked at the coconut in her hands, then at Bret as he raised his high again, and something clicked.

She'd never had so much fun pounding the husk off a coconut.

* * *

Bret couldn't help watching. As he broke his coconut meat into pieces, Kendal lifted her newly husked shell to her lips and gulped the milk down. She let it run down her chin and neck and . . .

He swatted at a tiny biting fly. They had both worked up a sweat, and the little buggers appreciated it.

Kendal lowered her coconut and wiped her mouth on her arm. "That was a really good idea."

He crunched on coconut meat. "I know a better one."

She looked at him in question, and he glanced toward the blue water just beyond the white sand.

She dropped her coconut and took off. "Beat you!"

He paused for just a second, watching her brown hair now streaked with sun flying behind her as she raced to the water. She was thirty-four and magnificent.

And she did beat him to the water. But not by much.

* * *

Why? Kendal pulled on a fin.

Why? She pulled on the other.

Lila knelt in front of her, checking her vest, chatting effortlessly with Craig, who sat on the edge of the dinghy.

"Okay, Kenni, I think that's everything. How do you feel?"

Kendal looked at her sister. "Why did I agree to this?"

Lila shook her head. "Because you've always challenged yourself? And you've been trained? And you want to see that sunken ship?"

Kendal stared. The RMS *Rhone* was an old, sunken British packet ship and one of the more fascinating subjects of her Google search history.

Lila took Kendal's face in her hands. "The water is crystal clear, bright with sunshine. It's only about fifty feet down, and you will be surrounded by people who care about you."

Kendal shifted the weight of the scuba tank on her back.

Lila continued in her enthusiasm. "Maybe you'll see a lionfish! Or a manta ray!"

"Or a shark," Kendal said.

Lila set her face. "I don't think the sharks in this area are big. Or aggressive."

Kendal nodded. But her voice quieted. "Why am I doing this? Shane isn't even here."

Lila took a deep breath and sat back on her heels. "Maybe that's why. Because Shane isn't here. It's just you. And look." She motioned to the beautiful blue-green water dancing with light. "No dark places, no cold. Wide open water to explore. You're in a giant swimming pool playing Marco Polo."

"Why didn't you ever certify for scuba?"

"Are you crazy? I live in Montana." Lila handed Kendal her goggles and moved to the rear of the dinghy. She was dropping off the divers and would anchor a little closer to the steep cliffs rising out of the water at the wreck of the *Rhone* and then would enjoy a gothic romance novel.

Kendal sat on the edge of the dinghy and watched Craig slip backward into the water. Dylan and Joe were already under, exploring the sunken ship. The dive would be the most ideal and interesting one she'd ever do—not too deep, lots to see of the ship's remains, and teeming with ocean life. That's why she'd agreed to do it. Because she would completely regret it if she didn't.

Bret was fastening a holster holding some sort of miniature spear gun to his leg. He looked up. "You ready?"

"Yeah." *No.*

He gave her a thumbs-up and put on his goggles. She did the same, making the seal good, then bit down on her mouthpiece.

"Breathe," he told her.

Finally, she took in a breath, the familiar sound of the tank filling her ears. He shifted next to her and took her gloved hand in his.

"Watch out for jellyfish—you don't have a wet suit on," Lila called.

Kendal vowed to give Lila a nice big wet hug when they got back. Bret lifted his fingers. One. Two. Three.

She fell back into the water and allowed the weights around her waist to pull her down.

As the bubbles cleared, Kendal took in her immediate surroundings. Clear water. Just like snorkeling. And a few jellyfish did bob along, but they'd be left behind at this depth. Bret watched her, and as everything seemed to be working as it should, she nodded, and he turned and dove toward the others. She gave him space and then followed. Every ten feet, they paused to depressurize their ears and regulate buoyancy. Below them, the sunken *Rhone* lay dead on the sand, enormous, stretched out, and unmoving. But the closer she came, the more she realized that wasn't true.

Most of the wooden hull of the ship had disintegrated over time, leaving a skeletal metal framework to explore. Almost 150 years ago, the ship had been thrown against the rocks in a hurricane and broken in two and, over time, had been claimed by the sea.

Almost every surface was covered in coral and sea sponge, anemones and water plants. The water was less clear down here, but visibility was still enough to keep Kendal's heart rate steady. She could see about twenty-five feet out, no problem. Blue-green water and algae created a base tone punctuated by bursts of red, acid-yellow, and electric-blue corals. Fan coral, tube coral, spires, and mounds of other vegetation created a vibrant cityscape for all kinds of fish. No, the RMS *Rhone* was not a still, dark grave. It was very much alive.

As the men chose different areas to explore, Kendal decided to follow Joe. Maybe because he was older, maybe because she judged him as less reckless, or maybe because he'd been to this spot before, but tailing Joe calmed her, and she found herself less concerned about breathing or how deep she was and more focused on seeing. He didn't seem to mind her company and pointed out things she may have missed on her own: the cannons, the crow's nest, parrot fish, triggerfish, eel, and even an octopus curled up in the shadows. Joe pointed out a silver teaspoon lodged in the coral.

It wasn't long until Kendal was thoroughly enjoying herself and, again, just like the snorkeling, wondered how she'd been so paralyzed with Shane. With her own fears.

After about forty minutes, Joe signaled he was ready to go up. But Kendal wasn't ready yet. He patted her arm and leisurely kicked upward. She turned and found a couple of the others. Dylan had cut open a spiny black sea urchin, and he and Craig watched as trumpet fish and snappers gathered to feast. Craig waved to her, and she waved back, then signaled the direction she was taking back around the ship. He nodded.

A bit nervous to be on her own but proud of herself nonetheless, she left the two men in search of Bret. She avoided a large grouper and swam through a school of yellow jacks. She found Bret taking pictures of an old staircase with his own underwater camera.

He saw her coming and motioned her closer. He moved to an area of the wreck she hadn't seen yet and pointed out a still, narrow figure floating in the water above them.

A barracuda. A shiver ran through her body, but she watched, fascinated. It wasn't a large specimen, only twenty inches, maybe, but that one eye watched them. She absently reached for Bret's arm and held on.

After a moment more, they left the barracuda to himself. Bret led her to a lone porthole, still intact in the metal hull, the glass clean. She'd read about the "lucky porthole" in her online searches. He rubbed the shiny brass and had her do the same. Then he took the hand she'd used and pressed it to his hand. She looked at him questioningly, their hands pressed flat to each other. Then he interlocked their fingers and held tight.

Good luck. Good luck for each other, she guessed. She studied his eyes through the water. He seemed very intent on her understanding.

She finally nodded, and he smiled around his mouthpiece. She laughed, and he took her picture.

Bret took more pictures, and Kendal explored nearby. The water had dropped a little in temperature since they'd started, but the sun still blazed above them, forcing its light through the rippling currents. She remained fascinated by her surroundings until at last Bret signaled that it was time to return to the surface.

They bobbed in the water alongside the dinghy, where Lila and Joe helped the others in. Kendal smiled. She couldn't stop smiling.

Lila caught it. "Have fun?"

Kendal nodded, saltwater dripping from her lips and lashes. "Yes."

"I think I'm going to scuba back to the boat," Bret said. "I saw some lobster down there I'd like to bring back for dinner." He turned to Kendal. "Want to come?"

She looked toward the *Wild Thing* balled about two hundred yards off. She nodded. "Lobster sounds great."

Using his spear gun, Bret caught two good-sized lobsters. He loaded them into his mesh bag, and then they headed back to the yacht. The scenery wasn't as exciting as it had been back at the wreck, but they still explored as they went, taking their time.

Bret spotted a school of snapper off to their right. He motioned with his spear gun, and Kendal understood he wanted to catch a fish to add to dinner. She stayed above him and watched. He caught a fish on the second try, and she clapped underwater as he held his prize. He added it to the bag.

An inexplicable shiver ran down Kendal's spine. She'd enjoyed herself in the warm open water, but there it was—the familiar beginnings of panic—and her stomach knotted. *Not now.* As she instinctively searched the water, telling herself it was nothing, three feet to her left something large appeared out of nowhere, and her blood chilled.

A reef shark.

It swam past her, intent, slow. About six feet long. The sound of her own accelerated breathing did nothing to calm her.

It moved on and made a wide circle around the school of snapper. And Bret.

They're not aggressive. They're not.

Her mantra fell flat. Bret saw the shark and paused. But then he readied his spear again. He was going after another fish? Was he crazy? His bag trailed a little blood in the water behind him.

She made a move toward him, not knowing what she could do, when another shadow appeared to her right. Another shark. This one bigger than the first. It moved on to follow the other.

The sound of her own breathing amplified in her ears, and her heart hurt with pounding. She kicked toward Bret at the same moment he saw the second shark. He left his second catch stuck on the harpoon in his hand and, after a glance in her direction, began swimming toward the boat. She followed him from above.

Yes. We need to leave.

The water seemed darker now, and though it was still warm, she shook and fought to regulate her breath. She kept one eye on the sharks and one on Bret. He was swimming faster than she was, and she wasn't sure he noticed that the larger shark still followed them.

They're not aggressive. They're not aggressive.

They look really aggressive.

He was leaving her. He was leaving her. She could barely see him ahead. She searched behind her, unable to see the other shark.

She pushed up. Kicked up. She broke the surface and tore out her mouthpiece, gulping in air, searching the water beneath her. "Lila!" she screamed. "Lila!" She gulped water and spun, trying to see, trying to find freedom from the dark water, from the darkness pressing in. She felt arms around her and heard the engine. The familiar dinghy engine.

Get me out! He'd left her.

* * *

Kendal sat on the top deck, alone, watching the sun go down. She'd assured Lila that she was all right. She'd smiled and eaten and played a game and then knew she'd done enough to excuse herself without worried looks following her. She was going to write in her journal. That had earned a look of approval from her sister, who no doubt believed some kind of therapeutic healing would be underway. The perfect ploy to be left alone. Her journal lay unopened. She stared at the horizon.

Silent until he was next to her, Bret sat down. She stiffened. She should have known one person would not be deterred by the mention of journal writing.

He didn't say anything for a long time. She wasn't going to speak first. She'd said everything she'd wanted to on the deck of the boat when she'd realized his arms were around her and she was back on board and they were alive and he'd been a jerk. She'd let all her anger loose on him, and he'd taken it.

Finally, he spoke. "So, what happened?"

Her eyes grew wide. "Excuse me?" She turned to him. "What *happened?*" Hadn't she laid it out pretty clearly after they'd climbed out of the dinghy? "You kept fishing! You took nothing into account for anyone else's safety or discomfort or fear . . ." The tears were coming, and she swallowed hard and breathed. "You left me there. You just

. . . left . . ." Okay, she had to stop talking. She shut her mouth and turned back to the sun, low in the sky. This would do no good, losing it emotionally in front of him. But anger coursed through her. What *happened*? She clenched her fists.

He paused, then lowered the bill of his cap, watching the deck under his feet. "I was trying to get away from you. To lead the sharks away. I didn't know . . . I didn't know the best thing to do. I didn't think they'd be any trouble. But then I remembered your fear and dropped everything. Dropped the stupid fish. I came back to get you."

She'd been told that. Lila had told her that. But she'd been too far into panic to realize. And too angry to let it ease her humiliation. Her failure.

Bret absently picked up her pen and began turning it in his fingers. "I asked you what happened. I meant, what happened . . . to the fearless contender I knew in college?" He raised his head, and she felt his gaze boring into her flaming cheeks.

Crap.

What she'd mistaken as callous, shallow idiocy was actually a quest to go deep. She couldn't look at him.

She turned away, studying the nearest island across the water.

"I apologize, again—"

She cringed. He had apologized. She knew it; he knew it.

"Because it obviously wasn't enough," he said. She took a breath to speak, but he put up his hand. "No. If you're still upset, then it definitely wasn't enough. But believe me when I say I didn't understand how bad I made you feel."

She turned to him. His gaze quickened, like he had to take advantage of her eye contact before she turned away again.

"I'm sorry. It kills me that I was so stupid and thoughtless. And that I made you feel . . . afraid." He clenched his jaw and didn't look away. "I would never consciously do anything to make you feel afraid." He gave his head a shake and looked down at the deck beneath his feet again. "I'm the guy who would have taken anyone down who made you feel like that."

And that, she knew, with the images of long ago shuffling in her mind—of their play, their competition, their companionship—was truth.

"I know."

He looked at her again, his gratitude evident. She nodded, and he breathed a sigh of relief, then looked out at the sunset.

"So . . ." She considered her words. "What was that, then? Where was your head with that shark?"

He dropped his chin, then mumbled an answer she didn't understand. "What?"

He turned to her, more determined. "I was showing off." He took a deep breath and said, "For you."

As much as she tried not to let it, a small laugh escaped her mouth. "You're an idiot."

He shoved her gently with his elbow. "Go ahead and kick a guy while he's down."

"Seriously, that's the stupidest thing I've ever heard."

"Cut it out." He shook his head and looked the other way.

She softened a little. "Okay, maybe not the stupidest thing. I'm flattered. Maybe next time you could grab the shark's dorsal fin and go for a ride."

He turned back to her. "Next time?"

"Still too soon."

He nodded. "I really am sorry. It was stupid. I've never had to impress you before. That's never what our relationship was about."

She hesitated but had to ask. "So . . . what's changed?"

He sobered and held her gaze. "I don't know. Something. A second chance."

She stilled. His eyes reflected the evening light, intense and searching. After looking a little too long, she turned away.

"You were always a force, Kendal. Strong, determined. The other day when we came up on that sinking yacht, I saw something fall in you. Things were pretty good until then. After that, you looked . . . defeated."

Slowly, she nodded.

* * *

Bret watched her search the sky. No makeup, suntanned, her hair shifting in the breeze, little curls forming here and there from the humidity. Lines around her eyes he found as attractive as the lean strength of her body.

She sounded resigned. "What do you want to know?"

"Only what you want to tell me."

"Liar."

He chuckled.

She nodded, smiling, he was pleased to see. "Fine. You're right. The sinking yacht."

He waited.

"That wreck made me feel . . . angry." She wrapped her arms around her knees. "Vulnerable all over again. The wreck was"—she chuckled sadly—"was my marriage." She glanced at him sideways before she continued. "You sure you want to hear this?"

"Hit me."

She went on. "I realized with Rick, obviously, that I wasn't crazy about him, and that wasn't very fair to him. We broke up; you and he graduated. A friend introduced me to Shane. He swept me off my feet. Handsome, charming, highly motivated, brilliant, incredible work ethic. People said we were made for each other, that I was good for him. We dated for a couple years, we agreed with everyone that, yes, we were made for each other, and we got married. And I was good for him. He suffered occasional anxiety attacks. He called me his 'calm in the storm.'"

"So he never saw you after swimming with sharks."

He immediately regretted opening his mouth, and she whacked him in the shoulder.

"Sorry," he said.

She smiled, then sobered. "Well, you're right. I did my best to hide that from him."

"Lucky guy."

Whack. "Ow."

"Well?" she asked. She still tried to hide a smile though.

"I promise I'll be good."

"I'd appreciate it."

After a couple moments, she must have decided she could continue. She took a deep breath and looked out at the horizon. "After we got married, things changed. Everything became about the business, about his career, about building our future. Long hours, weekends, conferences. I couldn't ease his anxiety anymore, and his resentment of that grew. Building our future soon felt like building his future, and I was set on a shelf and soon our daughter beside me."

Bret noted the change in her bearing, the way she folded into herself as she spoke of her ex-husband.

"To be fair, I don't think he saw it that way. I think he felt he was working for something. But somewhere, he lost sight of what exactly that was. He'd . . . put our marriage on autopilot. Set the course. Work hard. Work more."

Kendal ran her hand over her hair and watched the island lights blink on. Her eyes had become glassy. "You can't do that, you know? Changes come. Wind, current. Other pretty boats."

Bret frowned.

"And it wasn't watching the yacht so much that hurt. That was maddening, but it was worse watching the tugboat. That little, worn-down tugboat killing itself." She pulled at the neck of her shirt and steadied her voice. "That yacht kept sinking, taking on water, run aground because it hadn't been given the attention it required . . . and all I could see was that stupid captain, angry, blaming the tugboat for not being strong enough to pull the vessel off the rocks as it sank. For not being enough."

She turned to him, eyes rimmed with unspilled tears.

"You," he said.

She nodded, her jaw tight. "And I wasn't enough. So he found someone else. And he left me behind."

"Another tugboat," Bret said.

"No." A tear trailed down her cheek. "He found another yacht." She gulped in a breath, fighting her sadness.

He pulled her to him, wrapped her in his arms, and held her as she quietly wept. A woman's crying always unsettled him, and he'd always floundered in the comfort department, but holding Kendal was different. Their bodies had pushed, collided, run, and pressed on courts and fields. This was another hold. This felt like teamwork. She was down, and he'd hold her up until she could stand again, which, knowing her, wouldn't be long. He understood this kind of teamwork.

Eventually, she settled against him, calm.

"I hate yachts," she said.

He smiled. "So overrated."

"And sharks."

He chuckled. He'd never be able to make that up to her.

Color blazed in the sky.

She pulled away from him and wiped her eyes, sniffling. "Okay. What about you?"

He paused. "Now?"

"Yup. Hit me."

"Well, let's see." He frowned. "I'm a float tube."

Kendal's eyes grew wide.

"And I married a . . ." He thought a minute.

"A what?"

"A party barge, actually. Triple-decker. Lots of . . ."

"Drama?"

"Shoes."

She smiled. "Shoes are overrated."

"I noticed you don't wear any."

"We are on vacation. None of us are wearing much of anything."

He smiled. "I noticed that too."

* * *

Joe and Bev knew that on Friday and Saturday nights on the island of Jost Van Dyke, Foxy's Tamarind Bar served up a huge grilled dinner, music, and dancing beneath the thatch-and-T-shirt-roofed establishment. Kendal and the rest of the passengers and crew of the *Wild Thing* filled their plates with barbequed chicken, ribs, and mahimahi, as well as fruit, salads, rice and beans, and they ate a good portion of it at their long table, downed it with house drinks, and sang along with Foxy Callwood and his guitar. Foxy ended his session to applause and switched over to the DJ sound system. Kendal wondered if she'd ever consider "vacation" to be anywhere else.

Bret stood and bent down to Kendal's ear.

"Dance with me, Magic."

She laughed and shook her head.

"Now," he said with a grin.

She paused and looked at Eden, who shooed her away. Kendal finished her drink and took Bret's offered hand. Kenny Chesney crooned about sand and paradise.

Kendal had always felt a little out of place on a dance floor, as tall as most of the guys who usually bent over their feminine counterparts.

She'd never giggled and smiled demurely back up at anyone, and as she considered, she realized it had been a decade since music had compelled her out under a disco ball. What was she thinking wearing the little turquoise sundress, following Bret in his khaki cargo shorts and tight black AC/DC T-shirt, his short blond hair and reddish scruff and . . .

He drew her close and asked her questions, and she answered them as he moved her in a slow circle. And then they weren't talking anymore, just . . . dancing. And it was great.

Then he started singing, and she laughed, and he pulled her closer. And that was great too.

"What are you doing next week?" he asked against her ear.

She swallowed, her thoughts trying to make "next week" and "not being here" connect. "Um, working." Ugh, that sounded miserable. "And Mal. I'll have Mal back." That was better.

"Can I take you out Friday night?"

She pulled away from him enough to look him in the eyes. "Like . . . like a date?"

He shrugged and smiled. "Yeah. Like a date."

"But I live in Great Falls."

He chuckled. "I know where you live. It's not that far from Bozeman."

He was right. It wasn't.

Her phone rang. Malerie's number appeared on the screen. She pulled away with an apologetic look.

"I understand. Go ahead."

She smiled in gratitude and answered the phone. "Malerie, sweetie?" The music was too loud. Bret took her hand and led her away from the crowd, onto the sand near some tiki torches. And then he was gone.

"Mommy, can you hear me?"

"Yes, I can hear you now. How are you? I miss you so much!"

"I miss you too. I'm having fun. I can do a somersault in the water, and I don't get water up my nose."

"That's wonderful."

"And we went to Disney World! And I saw the dolphin show and the walrus."

"Oh, I wish I could have been with you."

"Me too. And, Mommy, I lost my tooth, and the tooth fairy gave me five dollars!"

"Wow, the Florida tooth fairy is giving the Montana tooth fairy a run for her money."

"What?"

"Nothing. Guess what. I saw a shark!"

"Whoa. That's awesome. Were you scared?"

"I was terrified."

She giggled. That giggle.

"Mommy, Daddy wants to talk to you, but I love you, and I miss you, and only two more days! Bye!"

"Wait, I love you too. Mal—"

"Kendal?"

She walked toward a log bench. "Shane."

"Hey, how's the trip?"

"Amazing."

"Good. Good."

"Five dollars for a tooth?"

He chuckled. "Yeah, sorry about that. I just don't get to see her enough, you know? She's getting so big. She's incredible."

The knot in her stomach returned. "She is."

He paused.

"Shane, this call is expensive."

"Don't worry about that; I'll cover it. Kenni, there's something I need to tell you, and I think it would be best to just run it by you now so when I see you at the airport, you know, it will be on our minds already."

She couldn't respond, just waited, holding her breath.

"Kenni, Cambrie and I are going to have a baby."

She dropped onto the bench and exhaled slowly, unsure what emotion to tag this information with. What was she supposed to feel? Or not feel?

"You still there?" He sounded nervous.

She forced out the answer. "Yes."

"Good. I know . . . I know this is not . . ." He blew out an exasperated breath. "Maybe I should have waited."

"You think, Shane? What on earth made you think we needed to discuss this right now?"

"Well, there's more."

She ran her free hand through her hair and braced herself. More what? Were they having twins?

"It's a girl. The baby's a girl. And I thought, I mean, we've talked . . . after having Malerie here—"

It hurt. It cut her like a knife, and that ticked her off. "Spit it out, Shane."

"Kendal, please. I didn't . . . I never realized how much Malerie meant to me, how much it would mean to me—"

This is it. Here it comes.

"And I'm asking you to consider giving me more time with her. To have her here, to be a sister . . ."

Kendal's knee bounced, and everything—the palms, the sand, the foamy moonlit surf—turned blurry. She bit her lip.

"You still there, Kenni?" he asked quietly.

Of course I'm here. I'm always here. Cables at the ready, engines running at max. Worn down, worn out, pulling as hard as I can. Give her a pool. Give her a sister.

"We can talk about it more later," he finally said.

"Shane?" Her voice cracked, but she was past caring.

"Yeah?"

"Why now?" She waited, her throat tight and dry as the tears pooled in her eyes.

"I don't know, Kenni. I'm sorry. Forgive me."

She lowered the phone, staring at it. *Call ended.*

Malerie's face grinned up at her.

The tears spilled over.

After some minutes passed, she wiped her face and stood. She turned and stopped.

Lila stood there waiting. "Kenni?"

"He wants more of Mal. They're going to have a baby."

Lila opened her arms, and Kendal let herself fall into them.

"Shh. Tell me what you need."

* * *

Bret watched Kendal leave the last-night party in the galley of the *Wild Thing* and go outside. She'd been quiet since the previous night at

Foxy's. Today had been their final full day on the *Wild Thing*. But she'd been cheerful and involved. She'd taken the helm quite impressively when they'd sailed back to White Bay on Peter Island. They'd spent the entire morning playing on rented SUPs and snorkeling. They'd followed lunch with jumping ship: running and leaping from the top deck into the water below. Eden was the surprise, going from absolute refusal to three leaps in a row and taunting everyone else. But nothing really surprised Bret anymore when it came to his sister. Like now. Eden wore a pirate hat and eye patch and was singing "Islands in the Stream" with Joe, who used a pirate hook as a microphone for their duet.

He found Lila watching him. She motioned for him to follow Kendal out of the galley. He gave her the "in a minute" signal, and she seemed satisfied.

Lila had filled him in on the phone call. He'd kept an eye on Kendal himself last night as her figure had become smaller and smaller on that bench. He'd given her space. But he'd had about enough of that.

The duet finished, and he applauded. As the others made the next selection, he grabbed two drinks out of the cooler and slipped outside.

He found her on the top deck, watching the waves. She turned when she heard his footsteps and, thankfully, didn't look upset. She motioned to the space next to her, and he took it.

"How're you doing?" he asked.

"I'm good. It's been a great day."

He handed her a drink, and she smiled.

"Old Jamaican." The closest bottled ginger ale they'd found to the stuff on St. John's.

They popped the tops, clinked their cans, and swigged.

"Not too bad," she said, squinting.

"No," he agreed. "Not bad at all." He set down his can. "Lila said you needed to talk to me."

She took another sip of her drink. "Yeah, I do." She set her can down and looked at him square on. "I need you to tell me why I should consider letting my ex-husband keep our daughter for a longer part of the year."

"Kendal . . . I'm not sure—"

"Bret. I've been asked to consider this. And for the life of me, I'm trying. But I'm coming up empty and clinging. To what is mine. To what I deserve." She took a breath to steady the quiver in her voice. "I need a different perspective. From someone I believe in. And that's you."

He watched her, wondering how he'd earned that honor. And wondering what kind of jerk Shane was to ask such a thing while Kendal was on a vacation like this. Bret reached and took her hand. Gripped it. "I don't want to be the bad guy."

She leaned her head to the side. "Neither do I."

He nodded and looked out at the water. He owed her. "It sucks. One day you're tucking your kids in every night; you come home from work knowing they're going to run at you shouting your name every time. You're calling them to follow you out to the shop so they can ask you a million and one silly questions, and sometimes you wish you hadn't called them to follow you . . . And then they aren't there. You wonder who's tucking them in, if they're getting the story they want. You come home, and it's so quiet." He swallowed and cleared his throat. "You wonder who's answering all their questions. If the answers are the right ones. If they miss running at you."

She squeezed his hand.

He took a deep breath and blew it out. "I don't know what kind of dad your ex was or is. But when I get my turn with the boys, I'm just scrambling to be everything to them in those few days that I can't be when they're gone. And most times, it's great. Sometimes it's a bust, but even then I'm just so happy to have them in my pocket again. And it's torture too because I had all that time, all that time before, and I wish I could just . . . get it back."

She watched him, her eyes red. He took another gulp of the ginger ale and squeezed his eyes closed at the sting. "Strong stuff."

"I wish it were a little stronger," she said.

He chuckled. He lifted her hand and kissed it, watching her. She didn't seem to mind. In fact, she leaned into him, and he put his arm around her.

He continued. "When they go home to their mom, I pray to God it was enough. That I'm enough. That I'm still their dad."

"You are their dad."

He met her gaze and reached up to brush her cheek. "I am. I want to be. And that has to count for something."

She nodded. "Okay." She took a deep breath and blew it out. "Thank you."

"You're welcome."

He held her gaze for a long moment. "So I'm not the bad guy."

The corners of her mouth lifted. "Not the bad guy."

They watched the sun settle low on the horizon.

"I'm going to thank Jay for getting sick," he said. "I mean, the trip sounded great, but when I heard you were coming, I couldn't pass."

She looked up at him, surprised. "Really? Because when I heard you were coming, I was ticked off."

He laughed and brushed her hair out of her eyes. "Why?"

"You know why."

"Yeah, maybe I do. That was a long time ago."

"It wasn't that long ago."

He looked at her and touched her face again. She didn't look away. He brushed the backs of his fingers down her neck, along her shoulder, down her arm. Her eyes closed.

"I can be the bad guy a little bit."

She smiled. "I do wonder about the kiss on the cliff wall."

"So do I. Often." He watched her mouth.

She opened her eyes. "If I'm remembering correctly, we're pretty good at it."

"I recall that, yes." He could smell her, feel her warmth.

She leaned toward him just enough to whisper in his ear. "The level of danger probably had something to do with it."

"Do you think?" Where was a cliff when he needed one?

She shrugged and pressed her hand to his chest. "Or maybe it was just . . ."

"Chemistry?" he offered, surprised he was still able to form words.

She nodded. "Exactly. There was definitely no harm in it."

"No," he said. "None whatsoever." He pulled her to him.

Just then the sliding door opened below. Eden's voice called up through the night as Bret and Kendal separated. His head spun.

"Um, guys? Sorry to interrupt, you know, whatever, but Bev made her Sinful Sundaes, and they're kind of awesome, so I don't know if you're interested, but they're down here with all the fixings, and these guys made me come out here to tell you. So, um, before the ice cream starts to melt . . ."

"Thanks, Eden," Bret answered. His heart pounded like he'd just run a marathon. The door slammed shut, cutting off somebody's wolf whistle.

"We should go down," Kendal said. But she didn't move.

He nodded. "Sinful Sundaes."

She ran her fingers up his chest. "How do you like your ice cream?"

He watched her mouth. "Really soft."

She nodded, leaning into his kiss. "Me too. Let's give it a minute."

"Or two." He pressed his lips to hers and closed his eyes.

* * *

Kendal woke up before dawn on their last morning on the boat. They would be sailing soon, bringing the yacht back around to Tortola and Soper's Bay. She quietly left her cabin and made her way up and out to the trampolines in the dark. She glanced at the hatch leading to Bret's bunk and pictured him there, asleep on the wall-to-wall bed he'd taken from her that first day on board. Out of obligation, last night they'd only lingered up on deck a short time before joining the others for ice cream. He'd squeezed her hand good night in front of everyone's expectant eyes. She didn't blame him at all and smiled now remembering Eden's "told you so" grin as she climbed into bed.

Kendal pulled one of the large buoys behind her as a support and settled into the mesh fabric to watch the sun come up. She'd had time to think. Time to consider. But her thoughts quieted as she listened to the waves and held her face to the breeze. A group of silvery fish jumped and flopped in the water, then were gone.

As the sky lightened, she heard the goats and smiled.

She felt stronger. She'd face Shane's request. She'd face the changes coming. She didn't have to fear anymore. She'd swum with sharks. And she'd survived.

The sun, not yet above the horizon, began painting thin stretches of pink and yellow on the clouds. The dark edge of the nearby island lit up, gilded.

Kendal sat alone, just her and the fish and the goats, the waves and the clouds and the light.

She heard the sound of a hatch lifting, heard the pad of his footsteps on the deck, felt the weighted shift of the trampoline beneath her.

He sat down. "Good morning," he said quietly and offered her a mint.

She smiled and took it. "Thanks." She popped it in her mouth. "Do you always offer a mint with your morning greetings?"

He had his camera on his shoulder and started fiddling with it. "Nope."

He aimed a shot at the sunrise and took it.

She leaned her head on her wrist. "And are you going to take pictures all morning?

He took another shot. "Nope." He snapped another, of her this time.

He set the camera down on the other side of him. "I'm going to spend most of the morning kissing you without interruption until you beg for mercy." He leaned toward her, his determined expression mixing wonderfully with his rumpled bed head and sleepy eyes.

"I'm pretty tough," she said, backing up a little.

He smiled. "I'm counting on it."

He reached for her, and she squealed. He hushed her, wrapping her in his arms. He'd had a mint too.

A goat bleated.

He lifted his head and called out, "Find your own mint."

She shushed him and pulled him back down to the trampoline. He tasted warm, sweet.

She smiled as her heart raced. They didn't need a cliff.

And she was not alone.

OTHER BOOKS BY KRISTA LYNNE JENSEN

Of Grace and Chocolate

The Orchard

A Christmas to Remember (short-story contribution)

Falling for You

A Raven's Heart

by Anita Stansfield

Chapter One
The Path

London, England—1869

STELLA HOLLINGBERRY FELT UNNATURALLY IMPATIENT as Patsy put the finishing touches on the sculpture she had constructed from Stella's normally stubborn-straight, ordinary brown hair. She had been sitting in this chair for hours while Patsy painstakingly used two curling irons, alternating them in order to keep them properly hot. Patsy knew how to use them perfectly in order to get the proper curl without burning the hair. Then she wove and tucked and pinned the curls until Stella actually appeared to be a real lady, someone who could fit into the life that presently surrounded her, the life she was trying so hard to become a part of—if only for the sake of survival. Stella knew in her heart—and Patsy knew it too—that if she had any other possible means to care for herself and this sweet girl who had been with her for more than a decade, she would have done it long ago. But options had slowly disintegrated, and only one possibility remained. Marriage was the only path that led somewhere besides the workhouse.

Stella had survived on the charitable nature of her deceased father's sister-in-law far too long. They weren't even related by blood, but Aunt Constance was the only person resembling a caring relative who existed in Stella's life. Constance had been very good to both Stella and Patsy since Stella's father's death a few years earlier had left her with nowhere to go. But Stella knew this could not go on forever, and she also knew what Constance would not admit: that her own resources were limited.

"So, this is it," Stella said, looking at her reflection as she clipped pearl earrings into place. Gazing into her own eyes, she felt like an imposter, and she sighed with all the resignation she felt. "I know Edward will propose tonight. I will accept, and . . ."

"Sentence us both to a life of misery," Patsy said with vehement cynicism.

"I was going to say that the matter will be closed, the problem solved."

"If you ask me," Patsy said, "you're just trading one problem for another. It's a mistake."

"I *didn't* ask you," Stella said, slipping into her red shimmery gown with Patsy's help. Realizing how sharp she'd sounded, she immediately added more softly, "Forgive me. This is just . . . difficult."

Patsy stopped fastening buttons down Stella's back and stepped in front of her, taking her upper arms firmly. Although they were close, and Stella knew Patsy was well aware that she could speak freely, Patsy still knew her place, and it was rare for her to be so assertive. "I know it's difficult, Miss Stella, but not nearly as difficult as it will be to endure marriage to such a man. You've told me yourself that you can see through his dupery. He's trying to find himself a pretty and vulnerable woman so he can inherit his fortune and get his parents to stop their nagging. And you're desperate enough to be that woman. It's doomed for disaster. I'm begging you not to do this—for both our sakes."

"And what else would I do?" Stella demanded quietly.

"I don't know," Patsy said, although she said it with conviction, not despair. "But we need to have some faith. I know you're in an impossible situation, but that's the moment when miracles happen. Just . . . have some faith. I beg you."

Stella didn't know what to say. She looked down, unable to respond. While she wondered where her faith had gone, she couldn't deny the truth in what Patsy was saying. Still, the situation felt impossible, and she'd resigned herself to doing what needed to be done.

Stella said nothing more to Patsy beyond thanking her for her help and complimenting her on the magic she'd performed with Stella's hair.

Constance was clearly delighted with Stella's appearance, and Stella just smiled and pretended she was thrilled to be going to this grand social event at the home of some very wealthy friends of Edward's family. Only minutes later, she was in the carriage with Edward, forcing herself to appear interested as he kissed her hand and spoke tenderly to her of his admiration and respect and his hopes for the future they would share.

They had been officially courting for several weeks now, and everyone in polite society was expecting an engagement to be soon announced publicly. Stella knew Constance was hoping for it, convinced that Edward was a fine man and a good catch. Stella didn't fear that Edward would ever be outwardly unkind to her. She had every reason to believe he would provide her with a more-than-comfortable living, and she even believed he would be a relatively decent father to their children. But she was having a hard time looking past the other aspects of this future before her. She knew he would not remain faithful to her, and she knew just as surely that he didn't love her. And she certainly didn't love him. If it was difficult to keep smiling through the course of a carriage ride to another part of the city, how could she manage to do so for a lifetime?

An hour later, Stella was surrounded by people she had become acquainted with through her time living with Constance here in the social nucleus of London. The sounds of music and conversation and glasses clinking had become brutally familiar. But the room felt suddenly stifling, as if remaining there might suffocate her. While she was looking around for an escape route to get just a few minutes of fresh air, she found her hand in Edward's.

"There's something I want to ask you," he whispered close to her ear, and her heart pounded. She expected him to guide her to some private hallway—or perhaps outside where she could get that fresh air—but he immediately used his forceful voice and commanding presence to get the string quartet to stop their music and to quiet the crowd. All eyes turned to them, and the silence became more suffocating than the noise had been a moment earlier. She had expected this to happen more privately, where they could talk about expectations and feelings, where she could at least feel like they had some kind of honest, mutual agreement in taking this step. If this was to be a marriage of convenience for both of them, so be it. And even if they both knew he would never be entirely faithful to her, she would prefer that they could be honest with each other, as opposed to the possibility of him lying to her about the kind of man he really was.

The next thing she knew, Edward had gone down on one knee, smiling at her as if she meant the world to him. She wondered if anyone besides herself could see the phoniness in his smile. The crowd gasped in unison, then all became silent again; apparently, each person present was expecting to witness a romantic proposal of marriage—like some form of party entertainment akin to a magician or a troupe of acrobats.

Stella heard the words come out of Edward's mouth. She felt his grip tighten on her hand and sensed the anticipation of the audience. The future from this moment forward flashed through her mind in perfect clarity. This moment was so typical of Edward. It would always be this way: his catching her off guard, using her to show off to make himself more admirable to others.

The tightening of his hold on her hand didn't hurt, but it seemed to convey a subtle threat: *Don't you dare embarrass me.* Or perhaps he meant it more as, *If you don't see this as the most wonderful thing that could ever happen to you, then you're a fool.* Perhaps it was both. Whatever his intention, Stella felt herself withdrawing her hand from his just before Patsy's words came back to her and the threat of suffocation became too much to bear.

"Forgive me," she said quietly to Edward, hoping no one else could hear. "I thought you would have the decency to do this privately so we could talk."

She turned and hurried away, Edward's stunned expression in her mind and the astonished whispering of the crowd in her ears. She couldn't get outside quickly enough, but she had barely managed to pull fresh air into her lungs before she heard Edward say, "I can't believe you just did that to me."

Stella felt immediately angry. "I can't believe *you* just did *that* to *me*!" she countered.

"I thought we had an understanding," he snapped.

"Not enough of an understanding to put me on the spot in public."

She heard him sigh loudly, then waited through a miserable stretch of silence before he said, "I . . . can see why . . . you felt put on the spot. I . . . should have considered that. I just . . . wasn't thinking. I'm sorry."

Seeing this side of Edward, Stella remembered why she had often enjoyed his company and had agreed to court him. But it didn't change what she knew she had to do. "Apology accepted," she said. "If it's all right with you, I'm going to ask your driver to take me home and come back for you."

"What are you saying?"

"I'm saying I want to go home."

"But . . . you don't want me to . . ."

"The answer is no, Edward. Forgive me, but . . . I just can't do it. I just . . . can't."

She was grateful that Edward was more speechless than angry. She felt sure he was confident he could put all of the embarrassment of the moment on her and quickly move on to greener pastures with the vast number of eligible young women who were looking for a wealthy husband.

As she let the reality settle into her through the time it took for the carriage to deliver her safely to Constance's home, she knew Edward would save face by resorting to gross distortions about her, which meant she could never hope to go back into these social circles again. Ironically, she was all right with that. And she knew Patsy would be too. She also knew Patsy would stand by her side no matter what. Perhaps they could find work serving meals in a pub. They were also both fairly proficient with needlework. She could likely make a decent governess; Patsy was certainly competent as a lady's maid. There were many options for women who were willing to work and many steps between the present and the workhouse. She had become so caught up in her belief that marriage was her only way out that she simply hadn't allowed herself to consider that she was not nearly as desperate as she'd come to believe. Perhaps society's views on the propriety of marriage as opposed to women applying themselves to an occupation had contributed far too much to her own perspective of the situation. Such options were better than condemning herself to a lifetime with a man like Edward. She could see that now. All she needed was faith.

Chapter Two
Faith

PATSY WAS UTTERLY THRILLED AT the outcome of the evening, even though Constance was understandably disappointed with the lack of a marriage on the horizon for Stella. But she was kind as she insisted that she would never let Stella and Patsy go hungry. Stella knew Constance meant it, but she also knew she was more generous than practical, and Stella couldn't take advantage of her generosity much longer. Still, as Patsy was undoing the laborious glory of Stella's hair, they formulated plans to look for work. Stella was amazed at how such a prospect felt so much easier than the social facades she'd been enduring, and she felt an enormous burden lift from her as she considered that she didn't have to marry Edward—or even see him again.

* * *

Stella's enthusiasm over finding suitable employment slowly waned through the following weeks. It had become alarmingly evident that opportunities for women to acquire gainful employment were rarely synonymous with *respectable* employment. She felt tangibly ill if she allowed herself to actually think about the possibilities of what might become of her, and when her sense of responsibility for Patsy combined with those feelings, she simply had to force such thoughts away and remember how Patsy had asked her to have faith. Surely something would turn up; surely a miracle would occur.

Not many days later, a solicitor by the name of Mr. Meath sent word through a messenger that he wished to officially call on Stella Hollingberry; Patsy declared with enthusiasm that perhaps this was the miracle they'd been waiting for. Stella couldn't begin to imagine why *any* solicitor might want to speak to her any more than she could imagine that a miracle could come by such means.

A few minutes after the stodgy Mr. Meath was seated in the drawing room with Stella and Constance, he surprised them both by making mention of a country estate many miles north, which was quaintly known as Ravensdale.

"You are familiar with the property?" Mr. Meath asked Stella.

"I have . . . heard of it," she replied. "If I recall correctly, a relative of my father owned it. But did he not die a few years back?"

"Yes. Mr. Ravensdale, your father's great uncle, left his property in full to—"

"His son," Constance provided with enthusiasm; obviously she recalled the incident as well.

"Adopted son," Mr. Meath corrected with disdain.

"Is that relevant?" Stella asked.

"In my opinion, such grand inheritances should be determined by bloodline, not by—"

"What exactly is the purpose of your visit?" Stella asked, purposely interrupting him. She didn't at all like his tone of arrogance and had no desire to hear his opinions on *anything.*

"No matter," Mr. Meath said, seeming to ignore her question as he furthered his own declaration. "This adopted son of Mr. Ravensdale, who went off to Africa or India or some such vulgar continent many years ago, has not claimed the property, and it has recently been discovered that he's dead."

"Dead?" Constance echoed in a tone that implied she had personally known him and might burst into tears.

"That's right," Mr. Meath said. "Dead." He repeated the word with even more drama than Constance had used, then he looked firmly at Stella. "Which means, Miss Hollingberry, that *you* have now officially inherited the property."

"What?" Stella and Constance both said in perfectly synchronized astonishment.

"As you know," Mr. Meath continued, "relatives in this family are difficult to come by, which is apparently why the old man must have felt desperate enough to reduce himself to . . . adopting a son, given that he couldn't have one of his own. Nevertheless, the point of the matter is that there is no other living creature who shares any relationship to the deceased Mr. Ravensdale. Your father is mentioned in the man's will; therefore"—he motioned elaborately toward Stella with his stubby-fingered hand—"it all belongs to you now. Although, I'm not sure if I would be so bold as to declare this to be such a good thing for you, miss; more a curse, in my own opinion. The house and grounds are in *terrible* disarray from what I've been told. Only a minimal staff there all this time, since Mr. Ravensdale's passing. There are more than sufficient funds to take care of all that and certainly money enough for you to live comfortably there, but I warn you that your inheritance is on the condition that you actually *live* in the home, and it's . . . well . . . it's in such *terrible* disarray."

Stella didn't fall under the spell of Mr. Meath's cynical attitude. Instead, she put all her energy into remaining self-disciplined enough to not jump out of her chair and let out a very unfeminine whoop for joy. Her own home! And money enough to live comfortably there! She didn't care where it was or how far away or how much disarray she might have to deal with. It was indeed the miracle she'd been hoping for.

She became lost in her imaginings of what Ravensdale might be like once she'd had fair opportunity to alleviate its *disarray* until Constance spoke and startled her. "Why such disarray, Mr. Meath? If there is a staff there and sufficient funds to care for the home, then—"

"The majority of the funds have been in probate, you see," he said, apparently assuming they both knew what *probate* meant. When he saw their confused expressions and an opportunity to explain, he ran his hand over his bald head and seemed to take pleasure in expounding. "Until the younger Mr. Ravensdale . . . if he could be called such . . . returned to legally make claim to the fortune . . . the will of the elder Mr. Ravensdale could not be finalized, which has left the matter . . . pending. Once you legally take possession of the estate, Miss Hollingberry, the bank will release the funds."

Stella asked a few questions, signed a few papers, and thanked Mr. Meath for his time. She was glad to have his high opinions and stubby fingers out of the house and stood holding the deed to Ravensdale in her hands, utterly speechless and overcome, as he walked out. It was Constance who brought her out of her stupor with a fit of great excitement as she called for Patsy and repeated the miraculous turn of events. The two women squealed with delight and laughed boisterously. But Stella just stood there pondering the deed. She wondered about the disarray of Ravensdale but, even so, was overcome by a strange sensation that she was going home.

* * *

As the hired carriage rumbled onto Ravensdale property, with the house barely visible in the distance, Stella's head stuck out of one window as she enjoyed the pleasant summer air, while Patsy's head stuck out of the other. The two women exclaimed to each other about the enormity of the estate and the beautiful countryside and the evidence that the land was neglected and sorely in need of human care.

"This land should be farmed," Stella said. "Much good could come of it."

"I'm certain you'll be able to put that right with time," Patsy assured her.

The two women and their baggage were deposited at the door of the manor house. They both stood looking up at the enormous structure in silent awe until Patsy said, "It doesn't look so bad."

"It's bigger than I expected."

They both gasped as the door came open and they were met by a stiff and formal middle-aged man who declared his name to be Warren and his position to be the head butler of the house; he would be the one Stella should consult in all things, since he was in charge of the household, and he would only answer to her. He was kind and respectful in spite of his rigidity, and Stella immediately decided she liked him. A man near the same age but quite opposite in disposition, with what seemed a constant smile and a much more casual dress, appeared to help Warren carry the ladies' baggage to their rooms. Warren introduced the other man as Harvey, who declared in a happy voice, "I do whatever no one else wants to."

On the way up a massive staircase, Warren and Harvey took turns explaining what time meals would be served and that the rooms where people slept and bathed, as well as the kitchen, were the only places in the house that were currently kept clean.

"It's just too much, you see," Harvey said. "O' course, the girls did a fine and dandy job o' cleaning the rooms for you, Miss Hollingberry, and your maid. Patsy, is it? We was told your name, you see."

"That's right," Patsy said.

"Your maid's room is directly next to yours, Miss Hollingberry," Warren said tonelessly. "I assume that will be satisfactory."

"Yes, of course," Stella said. "Thank you."

Stella was pleasantly surprised by the rooms. They were, indeed, very clean and spacious. But their décor was also cozy. And the view out of the windows was extremely pleasant, even if the land they could see had a wild look and seemed to be asking to be tamed.

The men left once they'd deposited the baggage in the proper rooms, and a few minutes later, two women came to the door of Stella's room, introducing themselves as Ethel and Nettie. Ethel was old enough to be Nettie's mother, and she was the head housekeeper. She made it clear she answered to Warren, but Stella could certainly come to her for help, and she would be happy to do whatever was required to put the home in order. "Oh, it will be good to see it come alive again," Ethel said. She had a formal manner about her, much like Warren, but her feminine tenderness came through, and Stella liked her as well.

Nettie was a housemaid and seemed a bit giddy over the excitement of a new mistress in the house. She said very little but was kind. And her enthusiasm over having the boredom and stagnancy of their household brought to an end was nothing short of endearing.

Ethel took Stella and Patsy on a brief tour of the house, at least enough for them to find their way to the kitchen from their rooms. They peeked into many rooms that proved Mr. Meath had been very right. The house was indeed in deep disarray. Not only was the majority of the house very dirty, but there were also some obvious repairs that needed to be done. The neglect was evident at every turn.

Once back in their rooms, Stella and Patsy helped each other unpack while they went back and forth between each other's rooms and discussed how their adventure was going so far. They both agreed that the staff they'd met all seemed very amiable, and Stella declared with a confidence that surprised even herself, "I really like it here, Patsy. It feels . . . right."

"I would have to agree," she said, and they exchanged a smile.

* * *

Dinner was served at a big table in the kitchen, where the servants had always traditionally eaten together. Both Ethel and the cook apologized to Stella for not having the formal dining room cleaned yet, which necessitated her eating with the staff. She was quick to declare that she would have no such division in her house.

"I refuse to eat all alone in some stuffy dining room while the rest of you are in here having a good time. I prefer good company and good conversation. I intend to work with you to put the house in good repair and then keep it maintained so we can all live here together peacefully."

Everyone except Patsy stared at her with wide eyes, then there was a pleasant chuckle that reverberated through the group, which eased the awkwardness.

Stella initiated conversation with each person present, wanting to know more about them, and she and Patsy in turn told them a little about themselves and how they had come to Ravensdale. They all seemed pleased when Stella expressed that she already felt at home, believed she would be happy here, and was greatly anticipating the opportunity to see the house and grounds come back to life. Supper proved to be pleasant, and Stella complimented the cook on her abilities, which made the woman smile and blush and express appreciation for Stella's kindness.

After supper, Stella met with Warren and Ethel to discuss the usual routine of the house—which she did not want to disrupt—and to talk about the most urgent needs in repairing the house and seeing the land put to good use. They gave excellent suggestions on people in the nearby village who could be employed to assist where necessary and some local farmers who would likely be eager to work pieces of land on the Ravensdale estate, according to typical local agreements, which would give them fair income from their harvests.

With some lists made and their meeting concluded, Stella asked Warren, "So, have I met everyone?"

"Everyone except Harland, miss," he said. "He takes care of the animals, oversees the stable."

"Why was he not at supper with the others?"

"Prefers to stay more on his own, I believe, miss. He's been here only briefly; six or seven months, I believe. A hard worker. Keeps to himself."

"And if I go to the stable now, would I find him there?"

"I believe so."

"Thank you, Warren. You've been extremely helpful. I'm certain we will get along marvelously."

"I would hope so, miss," he said, barely showing the hint of a smile.

She asked that he point her in the right direction of where to exit the house closest to the stable, then she headed outside, taking in the fresh country air, which was such a lovely contrast to the dirty air of London. She paused about halfway between the house and the stable to look up at the magnificent structure she had inherited by means that she had to consider a miracle. She could not get it out of her mind—it felt like home.

Chapter Three
The Legend of Ravensdale

STELLA ENTERED THE STABLE TO see a man, perhaps younger than she'd expected—likely near her own age—pitching hay for an evening feeding to four horses in stalls. At a quick glance, she also realized there were two cows, a few pigs, and some chickens. There were tools and tack that had obviously not been touched in years by how much dust and dirt had accumulated on and around them. But the animals appeared to be well cared for, and that was certainly the most important thing.

Realizing she had entered without being seen or heard, she took the opportunity to observe this man—her only employee she had not yet met. She still found it difficult to grasp that she actually *had* employees and, in fact, that she'd become an heiress.

The man she knew only as Harland had nearly black hair long enough to hang over his collar; it looked in places as if his curls were being forced into submissive waves and in other places as if the curls refused to be subdued. He was average height and average build. His clothes were simple, as she would have expected from a stable hand. But she couldn't ever recall being so fascinated with the fit of a waistcoat over a man's torso or the way the collar of his dirty white shirt fell open to reveal the muscles of his neck. A subtle quivering inside startled her to a feeling of complete surprise as she was forced to acknowledge where her thoughts had been. *Never* had she looked at a man that way before, and she'd barely gotten a glimpse of this man . . . hadn't even met him.

Stella turned slightly, tempted to leave and meet him later, but he caught her movement and turned toward her. She was nearly undone as the quivering inside her increased the moment she saw his eyes—hazel, she believed. A lantern hanging near where he worked compensated for the little remaining light of evening. She had a very clear view of his face, and her only thought was that with all the men she'd encountered in London, she'd never seen a face with such well-balanced features. But it was his eyes that fully drew her attention. They took her in as he absently set aside the pitchfork and removed his gloves, holding them in one hand.

"You must be the new raven," he said.

"I beg your pardon?" she said, entirely baffled by the comment.

"I've heard that for generations back the steward of Ravensdale is locally referred to as the 'raven.'" He took a few steps toward her, stopped, looked her up and down, and said, "You don't look like a raven."

"I'm only . . . related to the deceased Mr. Ravensdale . . . distantly, but . . ." At the evidence of her own stammering, she was relieved to hear him speak.

"That's not what I meant. I daresay you could only vaguely resemble a raven if you had just attended a funeral."

"I'm afraid black is not a favorable color for me."

"How refreshing," he said.

"You're Harland."

"I am. And you are Stella Hollingberry . . . which means that I now work for you."

"I'm afraid so, but I've been told I'm a relatively reasonable person."

"I've been told the same . . . although, I am committed to do whatever you wish . . . whether you are reasonable or not."

"I promise to be tolerably reasonable."

"I admit some relief to hearing that," he said and truly seemed to mean it. For the first time, Stella wondered if the staff had feared she might be demanding and arrogant and that they'd be forced to put up with her.

"Did you get something to eat?" she asked, and he looked confused by the question. "You weren't at supper with the others, and I just wondered if—"

"Yes, I've been well fed, thank you."

She found him looking at her with what appeared to be a deeper confusion. "Is something wrong?" she asked.

"I'm just wondering why you . . . asked, why you care . . . whether or not I had supper."

"I'm responsible for Ravensdale now," she said, and his confusion turned to surprise.

"The estate yes, but—"

"And the people who work here. If we're all going to share a home, we would do well to look out for one another, don't you think?"

He chuckled slightly. "It sounds perfectly reasonable."

"Do you mind if I look around?" she asked.

"It's your stable," he said and motioned with his hand.

She was well aware of him watching her closely as she moved about and took in her surroundings, trying to focus more on a mental list of what repairs and cleaning might be needed than on her temptation to be brutally aware of this man and the way he couldn't seem to keep from looking at her.

"The animals must keep you busy," she said. "Is it you who milks the cows . . . gathers the eggs?"

"Yes, ma'am," he said with perfect respect. "I make sure the horses are exercised each day and kept in good shape . . . on the chance that someone like yourself might actually one day want to use the carriage . . . or go riding. I've been working on repairing some fences, but it's been slow, I'm afraid."

"The care of the animals is most important," she said.

"Of course."

She continued to look around, not really seeing anything; she just wanted to stay here a little longer. She liked it here, and she liked *him*—even if she couldn't exactly figure out why. At this point, she could not credit what she felt to anything more than simple attraction, unless she could credit it to something intuitive that drew her to him. But she'd barely met him. For the moment, though, she just wanted to stay here and pretend to be fascinated by her surroundings.

"A raven is considered by some to be a symbol of good luck; it's a bird of magic."

"Is it?" she said. "And how do you know all of this?"

"The locals talk about it. The legend here is that if the steward of Ravensdale has the heart of a raven, the estate will always meet with good fortune."

Now Stella felt surprised. She looked at him, wondering if he meant more than he was actually saying. "And what do the locals say about the deceased Mr. Ravensdale who was steward over this estate for decades? Did he have the heart of a raven?"

"Most definitely. He's considered a hero, a legend."

"Then I have a lot to live up to." She looked around again, then looked directly at him. "What do you think, Mr. . . . I'm sorry. Is Harland your given name or . . ."

"Yes. Harland Leatherby."

"Fine name. What do you think, Mr. Leatherby? Do you believe I have the heart of a raven?"

"I would prefer you call me Harland. And since I've just met you, how could I possibly answer such a question? But . . . I'm leaning toward believing that you do."

"How very kind of you to say," she said and smiled at him. Then she realized that if she stayed any longer, she might make a fool of herself—if she hadn't already. "If you need anything or have any problems, please talk to Warren . . . or come directly to me. I want to do my best to make certain everyone and everything is well cared for."

"Of course," he said, fresh surprise sparkling in those hazel eyes.

Stella forced herself to head toward the door, saying as she passed Harland, "It was a pleasure meeting you. I will . . . probably come back tomorrow to see if I can . . . I don't know . . . do something productive."

"I will see you tomorrow, then," he said, and she hurried back to the house, pausing only long enough to look up at the structure in the dusky light settling over it. She realized then that large ravens were carved into the stone of the house, with some distance between each one.

Just before drifting to sleep in her new bed in her new home, Stella wondered if she really did have the heart of a raven.

* * *

The following morning, Stella took a handful of hair from each side of her head and pulled it back in a little ribbon, where it hung over the remainder of her hair down her back. It didn't necessarily look attractive or tidy, and it certainly wouldn't be considered very ladylike, but Patsy, who had carefully curled Stella's hair and put it up the previous day, was busy elsewhere. And even if she wasn't, Stella didn't have the time or the patience to be fussing with her hair today.

Stella had an early breakfast with the servants, which she enjoyed. Before the meal was over, each person had specific assignments for the day to begin the project of bringing Ravensdale back to life while continuing to keep up with their typical duties. Again, Harland did not eat with the others, and she wondered why. Only a few minutes after the meal was finished, she entered the stable full of energy and ready to see what needed to be done and do it single-handedly if necessary. She wasn't surprised to find Harland there, pitching hay into the horses' stalls for their morning feeding, but before she could even offer a word of greeting, he stopped suddenly as if a bucket of freezing water had been thrown on him and he was attempting to overcome the shock.

"Haven't you ever seen a lady dressed practically enough to work in a stable?"

"No," he said, implying that the word alone should offer plenty of explanation for his behavior.

"Is something wrong?" she asked, realizing he was staring at her.

"No," he said, but he didn't move.

"Let's get to work, then," she said.

He still didn't move.

Unnerved by his overt gaze, she hurried past him, saying, "Fine. I'll get to work." At that moment, she had to acknowledge her heart was beating quickly. She turned to glance discreetly over her shoulder, startled to realize his eyes had followed her and his stare remained firm.

"What?" she demanded, wanting to break this mysterious connection by her snappy tone.

"I thought your hair was curly," he said as though it should fully explain his odd behavior.

Stella's heart quickened further, but she focused on the variety of tools and tack she began tossing to the ground with the intention of cleaning every piece, as well as the places they were kept. Without looking his way, she simply informed him, "Not without a great deal of time and attention from my maid Patsy, and I haven't got time for such absurdities every day."

He made no comment, and when she finally dared glance in his direction, he'd returned to his chore so she returned to hers. They were the only two people in the stable for more than an hour, each managing to remain busy—and completely silent. When she could no longer bear the undeniable tension, she cleared her throat and forced herself to speak.

"It's funny how I have absolutely no difficulty making conversation with everyone else around this place."

He stopped whatever he'd been doing with the shovel and again assaulted her with that stare. "Are you blaming that on me?" he asked so nonchalantly that it took her off guard.

"You haven't said a word!" she retorted, sounding more defensive than she'd intended and feeling even more foolish than when she'd been trying to endure the silence.

He smiled with a silent implication that he thoroughly enjoyed knowing she felt foolish. "Yes, I have. I said I thought your hair was curly."

"Hardly a fascinating topic of conversation."

"Depends on how you look at it," he said, and she looked away. "What do *you* want to talk about?" he asked, much to her relief, and she was able to look at him again.

"Well . . . tell me about yourself. I've already learned a great deal about Warren and Ethel and Harvey and Nettie. And the other maids are warming up to me. But I know nothing about you."

He leaned on the shovel handle, and his eyes sparkled with humor. "So you haven't heard any gossip about me?"

"Absolutely nothing," she declared. He chuckled, and she added resolutely, not caring if he knew she'd asked the others about the stable hand, "Except that everyone else all agreed that you are kind and a hard worker."

He returned to shoveling. "That's a reputation I can live with, I suppose. Far better than things I've been reputed for in the past."

"And what might that be?" she asked, determined to have a *real* conversation with him as opposed to having the majority of their discourse based on her hair.

His hesitance to answer her last question made her think he preferred to avoid talking about his past. While she was considering a way to assure him that she would never judge him and he had no need to tell her anything, he said in a mildly terse tone, "I'm a different man than I used to be. I've come to appreciate very much what it means to get a second chance at life, but . . ."

"But not everyone agrees with such philosophy," she guessed with a degree of confidence.

His quick glance toward her made it clear she'd guessed accurately. "No," he said, using the shovel with more vehemence, "not everyone agrees."

"Do you think I'm like that?" she asked.

"Like what?" he countered, again stopping his work.

"So judgmental that I would not give a person a second chance if they sincerely sought such a thing?"

"Are you?" he asked.

"No."

He stared at her again, but she felt less uncomfortable now that they were actually conversing. Was it possible that Harland Leatherby needed his new employer's assurance that she would not judge him for his past or cease his employment if she learned something unsavory about him? She added an attempt at reassurance. "You don't have to tell me your story, Mr. Leatherby, but I truly would like to know more about you. And I promise it won't change the way I see you."

She heard him draw in a deep breath, and he leaned the shovel against the side of a stall. His eyes told her that what she had just said was immensely important to him. In fact, the intensity of his stare that had made her uncomfortable earlier was now magnified, and it took great effort for her to not turn away. It seemed as though his eyes were silently asking if she really meant it, and she was determined to show in her eyes that she really did.

"I may well hold you to that promise, Miss Hollingberry."

Chapter Four
Like Silk

"You are welcome to hold me to my promises," she said, "but I insist you call me Stella."

"I work for you. It would be entirely improper."

"And if I had not miraculously inherited this estate, I would likely be in a workhouse by now."

He looked startled. "Truly?"

"Truly," she said firmly. "There. That's the truth about me. Given that fact alone, how can I tolerate having the people who work so hard on my behalf referring to me as if I am somehow superior? Please . . . call me Stella."

"If I called you that in front of Warren, he would slap me up the back of the head."

This made Stella laugh, which had a contagious effect, and Harland laughed too. "Yes," she had to admit, "he probably would."

"So . . . when others are around . . . I will call you Miss Hollingberry. Although . . . would you be offended if I tell you that Stella Hollingberry is quite a mouthful?"

"No." She laughed again. "I'm not offended. I've always felt the same way. My mother always told me I was fortunate to be born a girl because I wouldn't have to keep the name forever, but . . ." She looked down and moved her toe over the ground, wishing she'd not made even the slightest implication toward such things. "I suppose we'll see," she concluded, then looked at him again. She purposely offered a silent challenge with her eyes as she added, "You know the truth about me. Are you going to tell me the truth about you?" She hoped he would. She couldn't deny her curiosity—or her fascination.

Before he spoke, she could see in his eyes that he'd made the decision to tell her—something, at least. "My story is a simple one," he said. "I am much like the classic prodigal son. I was given everything, and I threw it all away due to my own arrogance and selfishness."

Stella allowed herself a minute to take that in. She motioned with her hands to the disheveled stable in which they stood. "And what part of the story is this?"

"This is my humble willingness to work hard and prove myself worthy of all that my father gave me, even if it's lost forever. And I will do it with nothing but gratitude to God for giving me a second chance."

Stella actually felt tears sting her eyes, but she looked down to hide them. When she'd blinked them back and could be certain her voice was steady, she asked, "And where is your father now? Will you go home to him once you've proven yourself worthy?"

"My father is dead," he said, and she looked up, startled.

She hoped she wouldn't regret saying, "But the story of the prodigal son has a happy ending; he's reunited with his father, who rejoices at his return."

"I'm not expecting happy endings, Stella," he said, and she loved the way he said her name. "I just have to make peace with myself and hope that if my father lives on somewhere beyond this earth, he will know that I honored him in the end. Warren was good enough to offer me honest work for a roof over my head and food to eat. That's all I need, and I'm grateful for it."

Stella realized she was staring at *him* now, and he was staring back. His sincerity was so evident that he practically glowed with it. Something in his eyes made it evident that his life had been hard, some of it by circumstances beyond his control, she guessed, and some of it due to his own choices. Whatever his past or whatever the reasons for it, she was glad to know he was here now and that he was committed to starting his life over. She felt genuinely glad to be able to say, "Now that I'm here, you can actually be given a fair wage, as well as a roof over your head and food to eat. Perhaps when you've saved some money, you'll decide to move on and find—"

"I don't think so," he interrupted firmly. The implication of his words alone might not have meant much, but when she combined them with his gaze, she found it difficult to draw a deep breath.

Before she could think of what to say next, they were both startled out of their trance by Nettie's voice coming from the stable doorway. "Forgive me, miss, but you're needed inside."

"I'll be right there," Stella said to her. "Thank you." She glanced at the mess she'd made with her task she knew would take hours to complete. "I suppose I'll have to get back to that later. I hope it won't be in your way or—"

"Don't worry about it," he said.

She offered him a quick smile and walked toward the door. She had a thought and turned to say it, not as surprised as she should have been to find him watching her. "I'll see you at lunch?" she asked.

"What?" he countered, confused.

"I prefer that we all eat together. Lunch is at noon."

He looked down at himself. "I really don't think I should come into the house with—"

"It doesn't matter," she said. "You are a part of the household. Be in the kitchen at noon, or I will send Warren to slap you up the back of your head."

He chuckled as she walked away, and she heard him drawl light-heartedly, "Yes, ma'am."

Stella entered the house and was immediately assaulted with a number of questions about where she wanted certain things and how she specifically wanted certain repairs to be completed. She answered one question at a time, and Harvey agreed to go into town after lunch to order needed materials and make arrangements with a builder to take care of matters that were beyond any of their own abilities.

At lunch, Stella was pleased to see that Harland had joined them. As they all sat together at the big table in the kitchen, Stella delighted in listening to the conversations among these people who had worked together for so long. Patsy fit in well and was clearly enjoying her new home and the company that had come with it. Surprisingly enough, Stella felt much the same way. Only Harland Leatherby seemed a little out of sorts among the group, but as she discreetly observed him, she sensed that it was more out of some level of shyness—or perhaps it was a part of his own belief about being a prodigal. Did he not feel worthy to be accepted among these people? Even those of the serving class? Something in her heart felt warmed with compassion at the thought, and she instinctively knew it was true. She hoped that with time he would become more comfortable with his place here and be able to embrace his new life.

He was the first to finish his meal and get up from the table after he'd asked politely to be excused so he could get back to work. She told him he could go only if he promised to return at eight for supper. He offered a grateful smile and said, "Thank you. I'll be here."

"And tea is at four," she added.

"In the drawing room," Patsy informed him. "We might even have it clean by then."

"Thank you, but . . . I have a great deal of work to do," he said, seeming to believe that coming far enough into the house to get to the drawing room would be tantamount to high treason.

Stella kept busy in the house through the afternoon and found that she'd worked up a sweat by the time she sat down in the drawing room for tea. She was pleased that everyone in the household had taken her seriously when she'd invited them to join her. Everyone except Harland, who didn't show up.

It was after six that evening before she returned to the stable with the hope of making some progress on the project she'd started. She was ready to once again apologize to Harland for starting something she hadn't finished, which had left a big mess he'd surely had to work around in order to accomplish his usual chores. She didn't see him when she entered, but she stopped abruptly when she realized her mess had been cleaned up and everything was tidy and in perfect order.

Harland's voice from behind startled her. "I thought you had far better things to do than clean up what I've neglected to clean during the months I've worked here."

"I'm certain you've had more than enough to keep you busy. I just wanted to help put things in better order and—"

"I know," he said. "But that fence I've been working on has been broken for years. I figured it could wait one more day. A lady such as yourself has better things to occupy her time."

She laughed softly, glad to feel more comfortable with him than she had earlier. "Like beating rugs and scrubbing floors, you mean?"

His brows went up. "Is that what you've been doing?"

"Yes, actually." She laughed again.

But he was serious as he said, "I'm certain you don't need to do such things yourself. Surely you can afford to hire more help and—"

"Mr. Leatherby," she said with firmness but no condescension, "everyone presently working in the household works well together, and I believe it is more a lack of funds and perhaps . . . motivation that has created the present condition of the estate. The work on the land can be hired out; I'm working on that. But . . . as for the household, I prefer to keep it as it is. I will help get things in order; we'll get some repairs done. And then all will be well."

She noted that he was staring at her again, and she motioned toward the task he'd completed on her behalf. "It all looks . . . very nice. Thank you. I couldn't have done it so perfectly, I'm certain."

"I'm very familiar with where everything goes," he said.

Stella wasn't as much surprised with the comment as with the way he seemed—for just a moment—to exhibit some kind of self-recrimination at having said it. For a long moment, she thought about the possible reasons but couldn't come up with any.

"How is that?" she asked, careful to keep her tone bland.

"I've been here for months," he said, but he didn't look at her when he said it, and there was undeniably something tense in his manner.

Stella only wondered for a moment if she should pursue the conversation. Perhaps it was the way he'd stared so boldly at her earlier that made her feel like she had the right to be equally bold with him. "Mr. Leatherby," she said, "I would like to point out that you should probably never play poker because you would likely lose very badly."

He looked at her abruptly, astonished, very much like a mouse that had just realized the cat was on to him. She filled the silence by clarifying, "There's nothing you said that would make me suspicious, but the way you said it certainly arouses my suspicion—even though I can't even begin to know why. If I am wrong, Mr. Leatherby, feel free to correct me, but I would guess that you are hiding something. I am more than happy to give you a second chance but only if you are completely honest with me. I don't need to know your past—unless it's something that might affect your future here. I suspect you are not a very good liar."

He sighed, hung his head, then looked back up at her with resolve. "You are a very intuitive woman." He said it with adoration and respect.

Was her intuition telling her the truth about *that*? Trying to focus on one point at a time, she listened carefully to what he said.

"I am *not* a good liar. I tried to be for a very long time, but I could never get away with it. I am fairly good at pretending, however, and I've been trying very hard to pretend that I've never been to Ravensdale before Warren took me in some months ago."

"But you have been?" she asked compassionately as she considered the implications.

Stella watched him look at his surroundings with nostalgia as he said, "I was raised here." Looking at her again, he added with no hint of the discomfort she'd seen moments earlier. "My father was the stable master here."

Stella let that sink in and took a breath. "But you left . . . looking for something better . . . or different."

"That's right."

"And now you're back."

"Right where I belong," he said.

Everything he'd said earlier about being the prodigal made more sense now, and she found that her respect for him only deepened.

"Does anyone else in the household know?" she asked.

"Only Warren. He's the only one who was here . . . before. The stable hands all left when their pay was cut, so . . . he needed the help. At least my timing was good. He said it couldn't have been better because he and Harvey had been caring for the animals and he wasn't at all fond of it."

Silence fell over them, and Stella noted that he looked as if he were preparing himself to be struck. Did he fear she would send him away? She hurried to say, "Then your coming back was surely a blessing to all of us." She sensed his relief and added, "There's no need to pretend—at least not with me. All I ask is that you remain honest with me. If a problem comes up or you need help with something—whether it has to do with your past or not—just . . . tell me, and I will do what I can to help you."

"Thank you," he said.

She nodded and said, "That's how you knew . . . the legend about the steward of Ravensdale . . . and the heart of a raven."

He shrugged. "Well . . . the locals *do* talk about it."

She smiled and turned to leave until his voice stopped her. "You're not at all what I expected you to be."

She turned back to look at him. "I hope that's a good thing."

"Oh, very good," he said. "And for whatever my opinion might be worth . . . Stella . . . I believe that you do."

"Do what?"

"Have the heart of a raven."

"I suppose time will tell," she said, not wanting to show how his tender words—or his gaze—affected her. She smiled. "I'll see you at supper."

"Yes, ma'am," he said, and she hurried back to the house, wondering why she felt like the essence of Harland Leatherby clung to her as if she'd run through a spring shower and droplets of rain had left her damp from head to toe. No matter what else she tried to force herself to think about, she couldn't dry herself; she couldn't get rid of the way he infiltrated her every thought and her every nerve. She reminded herself that she barely knew him, and just as time would tell if she could live up to the reputation of her predecessor, time would tell if this attraction she felt to Harland Leatherby had any substance to it at all.

* * *

Weeks passed into months and summer to winter. It was much colder at Ravensdale than in London, and keeping warm in the large stone structure was a challenge that Stella and Patsy had to adjust to. Still, they had both come to feel very comfortable there, and they, along with the rest of the crew, had brought about much change already. Stella grew to care more and more for the people with whom she worked, and they had all come to feel like family. But it was Harland Leatherby who most occupied her thoughts. They saw each other at meals, and occasionally she went riding with him, which they did with the excuse of needing to exercise the horses. They had shared a great deal of conversation, and her respect for him had grown as steadily as her attraction remained firm. But she felt cautious and even uncertain. She had misjudged men in the past, but her life had also changed dramatically. She wasn't even certain she fully understood all that was expected of her as the steward of Ravensdale, and she couldn't honestly say where she wanted—or expected—her feelings for Harland to take her. A part of her just wanted everything to continue on as it was. With winter swirling around them, they were all fairly isolated and reliant on each other. And she liked it that way. She didn't want anything to change, but in her heart, she knew nothing stayed the same forever.

She walked through the cold toward the stable, lifting her face to the sun shining in an especially blue sky. She entered the stable, all bundled up in a way typical for her daily visits to the animals and the man who cared for them. There was more than a significant breeze blowing, and since she'd become accustomed to wearing her hair down and straight, it blew in her face as she walked. Once she entered the stable and closed the door behind her, she smoothed her hair back into place. She welcomed the heat from the fire in the heating stove that was always lit this time of day, but as she pulled off her gloves, she found Harland looking at her in a way that reminded her of their first encounters. They'd fallen into somewhat of a silent agreement to ignore anything beyond the comfortable friendship they'd developed, which made her feel as if he didn't actually work for her. But something suddenly felt different, and she wondered why.

Harland smiled as he stepped toward her, but he said nothing. She was astonished by the way he lifted as much of her hair as his hand could hold, then he let it slide slowly over his fingers while he watched it with the fascination of a child. Stella was too stunned by his impropriety to comment, but when his eyes shifted to meet hers, silence consumed her for an entirely different reason. Something completely indescribable and illogical happened in that moment, something she had never experienced before. She'd felt a glimpse of it when she'd first met him, but in the months since, she had efficiently kept every such feeling conveniently tucked away. What she felt now was completely unfamiliar, but she could hardly analyze the feeling when she was so taken aback with how long they had been gazing directly at each other, neither of them uttering a sound.

He finally spoke with a slightly raspy voice. "It's like silk."

"What?" she asked, disoriented and confused. But she couldn't bring herself to look away.

"Your hair," he said, still returning her stare. "It's like silk: soft and smooth and heavy, like a length of silk that might produce a beautiful gown—something a queen might wear."

Stella managed to absorb that he'd just given her a compliment, then a moment later, she perceived how profound and deep his compliment had been. Since no man had ever said anything so thoroughly sweet and tender to her before, she had no idea how to respond. Suddenly unnerved, she looked away, cleared her throat in a very unfeminine way, and said, "Not a curl or wave to be found in it anywhere, which makes it brutally stubborn."

"Like you?" he asked with a little chuckle.

"What?" she asked again, this time with more of a gasp, certain he'd just insulted her in order to balance out the compliment. But she looked at him again and found nothing but warmth and tenderness in his eyes. "Am I?" she asked, surprisingly calm; he had a soothing effect on her. "Brutally stubborn?"

"Only over the important things," he said, and she heard respect in his voice—something else she'd never received from any man. Before she could comment, he added, "With hair so beautiful, why would you try to force it do something it was not created to do?"

"What?" she asked yet again.

He chuckled. "What I mean is . . . why would you try to force any curl or wave into hair so beautiful . . . just the way it is?" He looked even more deeply into her eyes as if he intended some deeper meaning and he expected her to know what that meaning might be.

The moment she considered the possibility, she knew. In fact, she knew so clearly what he *really* meant that she gasped far too loudly for such a quiet conversation. But he smiled as if he felt deeply gratified to know she had understood his implication. She knew beyond any doubt that his comments about her hair had been intended as a metaphor in regard to herself. He might as well have come right out and said, *You are beautiful just the way you are.* The very fact that he hadn't used those actual words made it all the more stirring. She knew then that he was far more attracted to her than he'd been letting on, and she couldn't deny that she felt the same about him.

Chapter Five
The Unsuitable Suitor

STELLA COULD HARDLY SLEEP THAT night as memories of Harland's eyes filled her mind in a delightful but unnerving kind of way. The way he'd so boldly touched her hair—and the things he'd said to her—had stirred feelings she had been trying to keep properly at bay since she'd come to her new home. She felt like a fool to recall how quickly and awkwardly she had left the stable, muttering ridiculous excuses she knew he had seen through. She had been so overcome and confused that she'd declared to Patsy that she didn't feel well and asked that her meals be brought to her room. The truth was that she'd needed time to think, time to sort her feelings without interruptions, and above all else, she'd needed to avoid seeing Harland until she could face him and not behave like an utter fool.

After eating breakfast in her room, Stella concluded that all of this hiding would accomplish nothing. It had been hours since Harland's behavior had sent her reeling, and she had come no closer to understanding what to do about it. She concluded that they were both adults, and they ought to be able to talk maturely about the way they felt about each other. The thought terrified her, but she knew it had to be done. She declared to Patsy that she was feeling better and got cleaned up and dressed, determined to find Harland and talk to him as soon as possible.

Stella was more than dismayed to have her plan thwarted by the announcement that a man from a neighboring estate had come to visit her. She'd had very few visitors since her arrival here, and most of them had been futile attempts by people in the area to make her feel welcome. Once they had realized how nonconforming she was to typical society, it became quickly evident that they preferred to not be involved with her socially. Stella was fine with that, and she was grateful that her household seemed to be fine with it as well. She suspected that the same would prove to be true with this new visitor, but she still preferred not to be bothered.

Mr. Bernard Happer was at least a decade older than Stella and as stuffy as he was blatantly unattractive. She felt she had no choice but to offer him tea and put some effort into being politely social, but she had trouble not being distracted by her desire and need to be busy elsewhere. Mr. Happer seemed to have all the time in the world, and her distraction quickly led to boredom as he droned on about himself, then her boredom turned to frustration when he droned on about his family bloodline and their importance in the area, and finally, the frustration became anger when he made some not-so-subtle comments about her attire and the condition of the estate.

"Mr. Happer," she said, barely managing to conceal her true feelings in order to behave appropriately.

"Yes, Miss Hollingberry?" he asked, seeming to hang on her every word.

"It has not been so many months since I have taken control of the estate, and there is much to be done. In fact, I don't wish to be rude, but I wonder if we could continue this conversation another time. I have many responsibilities and—"

"It's interesting you bring up your taking control of the estate . . ." he said, his voice more high-pitched than most men's. "Word is going around that there is some question as to the validity of the will."

Stella kept herself from making a horrified noise and was proud of herself for her perfect dignity as she said, "My solicitor assured me that everything was in perfect order."

"Perhaps you should check with him again," Mr. Happer said, finally standing to leave, "just to be sure." He said it as if he'd just told her a joke; he laughed with a snort while Stella escorted him to the door, making no effort to be polite enough to ask him to return.

Stella was dismayed to realize her motivation to speak with Harland had completely disappeared. She couldn't face him while she was so thoroughly distracted by Mr. Happer's untimely visit. So she returned to her room and declared to Patsy that she didn't feel very well after all.

Through the remainder of the day, Stella tried to convince herself that Mr. Happer—and whatever gossip he might have heard—were simply wrong. But after a sleepless night, she sought out Warren at the first opportunity and repeated what Mr. Happer had said.

"Mr. Happer's father and the elder Mr. Ravensdale were very good friends for many years. His name *was* mentioned in the will, but it surely would have nothing to do with the estate. And since the elder Mr. Happer is also deceased, it is surely irrelevant. I'm certain Mr. Meath would not have contacted you if he had not been absolutely certain of the legality. He is very thorough."

"Thank you," she said, realizing how she'd grown to love Warren's formal manner and precision in all he did. She'd grown to love everything about Ravensdale and all of the people here. She prayed that Mr. Happer was as wrong as Warren seemed to think he was, but the very mention that the man's father had been cited in the will at all made her nervous. Before lunch, she wrote a letter to Mr. Meath and sent Harvey into town to have it posted to London right away. Of course, she had no idea how long it would take for the letter to arrive and for her to receive a response, but she could only pray that all would be well and that Mr. Happer was nothing more than an annoying busybody trying to stir up trouble.

With that taken care of as much as it could be for the moment, Stella finally found the nerve and the courage to go out to the stable, having no idea what she might say or what might happen. She only knew she couldn't hide from Harland—or these feelings—any longer.

Taking especially slow steps between the house and the stable, she considered all she knew about him. She had no reason to believe he wasn't trustworthy. He was certainly dependable and worked hard. He was kind and warm—not only with her but with everyone. He treated people with respect, and that was important to her. Through their many conversations, he had proven himself to be wise and insightful, and his views on the matters of greatest importance in this life were based in a foundation of faith and integrity. By the time she got to the stable door, she had to admit that she had nothing to fear about him—except her feelings about him, perhaps. She simply had no idea how to handle this and could only hope he did.

She wished the weather was warmer and the stable door was open, which would make her arrival more discreet. As it was, she couldn't hope to enter undetected as she pushed open the noisy door, then closed it again. In the time it took her to do so, Harland had obviously stopped whatever chore he'd been busy at and was just standing there looking as though he'd been waiting in that exact place since she'd last walked out.

"Feeling better?" he asked with only a hint of sarcasm.

"It's difficult to say," she admitted. "My . . . ailment wasn't really . . . physical."

"Really?" he said, his sarcasm deepening. "I never would have guessed." He put his hands on his hips, and she wondered if he was angry. "You run out of here like a frightened mouse, and then I don't see your face for two days."

Stella looked away, searching for the right words. "I . . . needed time . . . to think." She knew she had to be honest. "What you said . . . startled me." She found the courage to look at him again. "Or maybe it was the way you said it." When he said nothing for a string of seconds that felt like as many minutes, she added in a voice that had more bite to it than she'd intended, "What?"

"I'm just trying to figure out why you would be *startled* by what I said—or how I said it—when you know very well how I feel." Stella wanted to ask for a clarification; she wasn't sure she *did* know. But he hurried on. "I have given the matter time for obvious reasons, but the way we feel about each other is not going to change, Stella."

Her heart quickened, then it began to pound as he moved toward her. She felt like she needed to say something—do something. But what? She wanted to declare perfect ignorance and pretend she had no idea what he was talking about. But he would see through that. She wanted to run back to her room and hide for another day or two. Or maybe a week. But his words rang with truth through her mind. *The way we feel about each other is not going to change.*

Their eyes connected, and she was taken back to how he'd looked at her exactly that way when they'd hardly known each other many months ago. Now they knew each other well, but that look in his eyes was the same.

"Stella," he whispered and touched her face, which prompted a tingling in her skin.

When she could hear herself breathing, she felt certain he could hear her too. She then realized he intended to kiss her, and she felt both terrified and thrilled. No man had ever kissed her lips before, and she allowed the terror to override the thrill.

"Please," she said, reluctantly putting her fingers over his lips to stop him. "We . . . mustn't."

"Why not?" he asked, his voice low and husky.

"I . . . have an obligation . . . to . . . this land . . . these people." As the words came out of her mouth, she wondered why she'd even said them. Her nervousness was prompting her to act like a fool again, but she didn't have the presence of mind to correct the statement.

"And you can't fill that obligation married to the stable boy?"

She gasped. "Who said anything about marriage?"

"Do you think I would have tried to kiss you if I weren't already hopelessly in love with you?" She gasped again while they shared a long gaze, which gave his eyes the opportunity to repeat what he'd just admitted. While Stella could hardly breathe, he added gently, "And you will never convince me that you don't feel the same. You must promise me you will never play poker because you would lose very badly."

It took Stella a long moment for the full implication of his words to get past the shock they had created in her mind. She turned her back abruptly and found it difficult to draw sufficient breath.

"Are you afraid of what the people of polite society in the area would think if you married beneath you?"

"I care nothing of what they think," she declared hotly, putting a hand to her chest as if that might aid her struggle to breathe normally.

"You, who shares every meal with your servants and works alongside them at all hours, do not have to tell me that."

"Then why did you ask?"

"To get you to say it," he said. "So if that's not it, you must consider me unsuitable because you're afraid I would only be interested in marrying you for your money."

She knew it wasn't true, but she felt compelled to state a fact. "You cannot deny that according to all things legal, everything I have would become yours if I were to marry you."

"I cannot deny it," he said, and he took a step closer. She gasped to feel his chest against her back and gasped again when his hands took hold of her shoulders. He lowered his voice to a whisper that tickled her ear. "Stella . . . do you really believe that's the kind of man I am?"

"No," she admitted on a long, slow breath and found herself leaning back against him, loving the way his strength seeped into her. She felt truly safe and secure.

"You're an intelligent woman, Stella, with good instincts and a strong intuition. I know that well enough. You have to be smart enough to use your brain, but you can't let your thinking overpower what you feel in your heart." She felt more than heard him draw a deep breath before he added, "Marry me, Stella." She gasped again. He added with firm resolution, "Trust me when I tell you that whatever may or may not be true about you or me or anything going on around us, I love you, and nothing is more important to me than you and your best interests. I will devote my life to making you happy and taking very good care of you."

Stella was far too stunned and breathless to know what to say. As helpless as she felt, she was glad for the way he gently turned her to face him and took hold of her shoulders again. Looking into his eyes now, with his proposal of marriage hovering in the air around them, Stella felt the warmth of tears brimming in her own eyes. Still, she didn't know what to say. When she'd come out here, ready to talk to him about whatever might be going on, she had never expected *this*.

"Would you like some time to think about it?" he asked, and she felt rescued by his ability to know how she was struggling for words.

"Yes, please," she managed, her voice quivering.

"Take all the time you need," he said. "I will never stop loving you."

His sincerity forced Stella's tears to swell in her eyes to a point that she knew he would see them clearly. He only touched her face again and asked in little more than a whisper, "May I kiss you now? Heaven knows I've wanted to since the moment I laid eyes on you."

"You have?" she asked in wonder, trying to imagine such thoughts in his head during their first encounters.

"Oh yes!" he said with quiet vehemence and didn't wait for permission before he bent slowly toward her and touched his lips to hers. His kiss lasted longer than she'd expected, most likely because she felt certain such moments happened only in fairy tales. She'd never experienced anything so perfectly blissful, and she wanted it to go on forever. But suddenly, it was over, and she was looking into his eyes again, wondering what to say. She felt something akin to panic when he took a step back and said, "Take all the time you need, but try to be merciful enough to remember I will be counting the hours."

He went back to work as if nothing out of the ordinary had taken place, and Stella went back into the house and straight to her room, where she wept for more than an hour, grateful not to be caught at it. When her tears settled, she felt surprisingly calm. She *did* need time . . . to be sure. But she felt a deep peace at the thought of spending the rest of her life with this man who was perhaps more at home here at Ravensdale than she was. It just felt right.

The remainder of the day went on as if nothing had changed, but Stella felt like a completely different person. She found it difficult to keep a straight face while sitting at the same table with Harland, there among the others, to share a meal. More than once they exchanged a discreet smile, and she saw something hopeful in his eyes that mirrored her own feelings. She slept better that night, and at breakfast, she could almost believe everything was as it had always been—except that now she fully understood that look in Harland's eyes and she knew the implication of his discreet smiles aimed toward her when no one was watching. She felt giddy as she walked out to the stable later that morning, just as she'd done practically every day since she'd come here. She wondered if he would be as polite and discreet with her privately as he had been publicly—at least until she gave him an answer. But the moment she came through the door, he dropped what he was doing, took her in his arms, and kissed her in a way that made yesterday's kiss pale in contrast. Stella laughed, and he kissed her again before he admitted, "Oh, I wanted so badly to do that at breakfast!"

She laughed again. "That would have caused quite a stir."

"You just wait," he said, kissing her once more, "I may yet cause quite a stir around here."

"I do hope so," she said and settled her head on his shoulder, loving the feel of his arms around her. She realized then that she too had wanted this since the moment she'd first laid eyes on him, but since she'd never experienced such a thing, she'd not been able to define what exactly she'd wanted. She quietly told him she needed more time to consider his proposal, but she reassured him that she was hopeful it would all work out. They agreed to remain discreet in the meantime, and she forced herself to leave so they could both get something accomplished.

* * *

Less than a week after Stella sent her letter to London, Mr. Happer called on her again, this time boldly telling her he had consulted with a professional who had seen the final will and testament of the elder Mr. Ravensdale. "I have been advised that if the language is studied carefully, it is clear that my father may well have inherited the whole of Ravensdale and that there is a very good chance it clearly implies I should be the sole beneficiary in my father's absence."

Stella was astonished but kept her growing temper in check. "Mr. Happer," she said, "first of all, might I point out that the term *clearly implies* is an oxymoron, which I suspect would also describe your ridiculous efforts to try to create a discrepancy where I am certain none exists. I do not know your motives, Mr. Happer, but I have written to my solicitor, and he will clear all of this up right away. You may leave now."

"Miss Hollingberry," he said, again using her name as if he were besotted with her when everything else he'd ever said to her had either been arrogant or blatantly rude, "there is another possible solution to all of this."

"And what might that be?" she snapped.

He took a step toward her and took her hand. She stepped abruptly back and drew her hand away, feeling like she had come in contact with some kind of reptile. "Mr. Happer!" she said. "You'd do well to mind your manners."

"Don't be so coy, my dear," he said.

"*My dear?*" she retorted, sounding as angry as she felt. "There is *nothing* in our relationship that gives you any right to call me such a thing or to expect what you are implying."

She felt unnerved by the way he remained so cool; he even smiled, apparently unaffected by her reproach, and said somewhat smugly, "You might come to see things differently when the truth comes to light. Even your Mr. Meath cannot dispute the true meaning of the will. But . . . if you were to marry me—"

"Not as long as there is breath in me!" she snarled. "Now get out of my house!"

He moved toward the door but still seemed unaffected by anything she had said. "If all you have here is so precious to you, I wonder what lengths you would go to in order to preserve it."

For minutes after Mr. Happer left, Stella paced the hall, fuming and afraid. What if he was right? What if she had to leave it all behind? What if these people who relied on her were suddenly in the care of an arrogant snob like Mr. Happer? The thought made her sick to her stomach. And when she thought of Harland and what this would mean to him and his future, the sickening feeling heightened.

Chapter Six
The Raven's Heart

HOURS PASSED BEFORE STELLA FOUND the courage to go talk to Harland about Mr. Happer's threats and how deeply concerned she felt. The moment she walked into the stable, she could tell his mood was foul.

"Is something wrong?" she asked.

"You tell me," he said and kept working.

"I would prefer you just tell me what you're upset about, as opposed to playing some kind of guessing game."

"Fine," he said and tossed the pitchfork and crossed his arms over his chest before he faced her. "I hear Mr. Happer proposed marriage."

"My goodness," she said, now angry herself. "Gossip spreads quickly around here. But allow me to clear up an important point. Mr. Happer did not *propose* anything. He *threatened* me with the possibility of losing everything if I did not accept."

"What?" Harland demanded, his mood immediately changing from anger to astonishment. "How is that possible?"

She quickly repeated everything the auspicious Mr. Happer had said to her. Harland listened and made no comment, although she sensed he wanted very much to say plenty but was exercising great self-discipline to remain quiet. When she had nothing more to tell him, she expected him to reassure her that it had to be a mistake and surely this man's threats were meaningless. She certainly *wanted* such reassurance. But he only asked, "So what will you do?"

"What will I *do*?" she echoed.

"*Will* you marry him to sacrifice yourself for Ravensdale and the people here you've grown to care for—for whom you feel responsible?"

"That question is irrelevant," she said. "I'm certain there is nothing to be concerned about."

"But what if it's true?" he demanded. "What if?" He sounded angry again. "That's what I want to know. Would you choose *him* over *me* to save this place?"

Stella was startled to realize she couldn't give him a firm answer. She turned her back to him and admitted, "I honestly don't know."

"You cannot be serious!" he growled. "I cannot believe with all you and I feel for each other, not to mention simply knowing the kind of woman you are, that you would even *consider* such an absurd option! And let me assure you that not *one* of the people who lives and works here would *ever* want you to consider such an option. In truth, they would be disappointed in you to know you even gave it a second thought. *If* his theories have any truth to them—which I seriously doubt—I would hope you have enough self-respect to make the right choice."

Stella thought about that for a long minute, then turned toward him, speaking in a soft voice that took him off guard. "And tell me, Harland, which choice would a woman make who truly has the heart of a raven? Would she walk away from Ravensdale with her *self-respect* and leave it all in the hands of an arrogant fool? Or would she sacrifice everything she has to preserve what has been entrusted to her?"

He said nothing, and she wanted to drop to her knees and sob like a child, so she hurried back to the house, praying with all her heart and soul that there was no truth to Mr. Happer's theories and this would all clear up before it created any more drama or turmoil.

* * *

For days, Stella avoided Harland, except for at mealtime when she tried not to make eye contact with him. Mr. Happer came to call, but Warren sent him away at Stella's request. Warren reassured her that she had no need to speak with him if she didn't wish to. He also told her that if Mr. Happer truly had any legal claim, he would send a solicitor to take care of the matter, and Mr. Meath would be her advocate. This made her feel a little better, but she still hadn't heard from Mr. Meath, and she could hardly even think straight while she wondered what the outcome might be and what she should do if she had no choice but to face the worst.

The following evening after supper, Stella was about to change for bed when Ethel came to tell her Mr. Meath had just arrived and wished to speak with her.

"He's here?" Stella exclaimed. She'd been watching the post for some word from him, but she'd not expected him to travel all this way. While she was thrilled at the prospect of having an advocate, his coming here implied that the matter was perhaps more serious than she'd been willing to accept.

"He's in the library, miss," Ethel said, and Stella hurried downstairs to speak to him, fighting to quell her nerves.

She entered through the open door to find Mr. Meath sitting at the desk, writing vigorously. She could well imagine that he filled every spare moment with work. He barely glanced up at her as he said, "Hello, Miss Hollingberry."

"Hello," she said, noting that Warren was standing nearby like some kind of sentinel. And she wondered if he was here to aid Mr. Meath or herself. She leaned more toward the latter when she turned and realized that Mr. Happer was sitting in the room, wearing a smug expression that provoked nausea on Stella's part.

"What are you doing here?" Stella demanded of him.

"Your solicitor summoned me," he said.

"Indeed I did," Mr. Meath said and set down his pen. He then leaned back in his chair, looked directly at Mr. Happer, and added firmly, "I do not know where you came up with this ridiculous notion that you might have any right to this estate or what kind of *professional* might have advised you to believe that such might be the case, but it's hogwash!" Mr. Meath rose to his feet in a sudden burst of anger. "You send this *professional* to me, and we will settle it rightly. Now get out of here, and don't show your face at Ravensdale ever again."

Mr. Happer argued his case rather vehemently to Mr. Meath for a good many minutes, until it became evident that Mr. Meath would not be affected, nor would he be swayed. When it was clear Mr. Happer had absolutely nothing legal to stand on and his wounded pride would only become more so the longer he stayed, he scurried away like a frightened rabbit. Before Stella could even take in her delight and relief, her admiration for Mr. Meath increased dramatically. She had stewed over this for so many days, and now it had all been washed away so quickly. She could only say, "Thank you, Mr. Meath, for—"

"There is another matter we must discuss," he said as if the matter of Mr. Happer was insignificant.

"Very well," she said, feeling nervous again. She reluctantly sat down, fearing her knees might fail her otherwise. Mr. Meath looked directly at her, and she saw compassion in his eyes, as if he was about to tell her a loved one had died. She didn't know him well, but this seemed out of character for him. Her heart quickened with dread, and she wondered what could be so serious. She braced herself to remain dignified and take the news gracefully—whatever it might be.

"Mr. Warren has informed me," Mr. Meath said, "that the younger Mr. Ravensdale is alive and well after all."

It took Stella several moments to digest what this meant. "I see," she managed to say and forced herself to remain composed. "Is he . . . a good man? He'll . . . take good care . . . of Ravensdale?"

Mr. Meath looked at Mr. Warren to provide the answer. "He is, yes," Warren said.

Mr. Meath then said to Stella, "There is no need to be concerned for your future. You will be more than sufficiently provided for. There is just the matter of some paperwork, and . . . Mr. Warren? Will you bring him in?" He nodded toward the butler, who walked into the hall, and Stella's heart pounded painfully. She didn't have to be concerned over the welfare of this beloved place or its residents, but she would have to leave it all behind after she'd come to love it so dearly. And now she was apparently going to come face-to-face with the presumed-dead Mr. Ravensdale. She could hardly breathe.

Then she couldn't breathe at all when she looked up to see Mr. Warren standing directly in front of her, with Harland Leatherby at his side.

"Forgive me," Harland said to her before she'd even been able to grasp the implication. "I will explain everything later, but . . . you must know I just felt so . . . unworthy of everything he left to me. He adopted me when I was left orphaned. He gave me everything, even his name, and I threw it all away. I truly believed Ravensdale would be better off in someone else's hands, but . . . I had to stay close . . . I had to be sure."

Stella could only stare at him as she desperately tried to put all the pieces together in her mind. She wanted to both slap him and throw her arms around him and hold him close.

"I had every intention," Harland went on, "of telling you once you'd accepted my proposal—*if* you accepted. But then this . . . Mr. Happer business stirred everything up. I have no idea how—"

"I must confess," Warren said, "that part is my doing. I am the one who started the rumor about the possibility of the will being in Mr. Happer's favor, and the professional he spoke to is a longtime acquaintance of mine."

"Warren!" Harland said in a scolding voice that made it easier for Stella to see him as lord of the manor. "You sly dog," he added with a trace of humor.

The butler smiled. "I was growing terribly impatient with all of this meandering about." He made a comical gesture with his hand. "And I knew Mr. Meath would set things right soon enough."

"And so he did," Harland said, again looking at Stella.

"This is ready for you to sign, Mr. Ravensdale," Mr. Meath said as if he'd been waiting for his cue or, perhaps, more likely waiting for all of the tedious explanations to be done so he could get on with his business.

"Thank you, Mr. Meath," Harland said and walked to the desk, where he leaned over, glanced at the document, and took up a pen.

"Are you absolutely certain?" Mr. Meath asked him, and their eyes met briefly.

"Absolutely," Harland said and signed a name Stella realized was much longer than the one she knew him by. Mr. Meath then asked Warren to sign his name to the document, witnessing the identity of Mr. Ravensdale as well as his being present at the signing.

Warren then left the room, and Mr. Meath rolled up the document and handed it to Harland as he came to his feet, declaring heartily, "My business here is done, but Ethel has kindly offered me supper and a room for the night, and I am going to take advantage of a good meal and a good night's sleep before heading back to London. I hope to see you again soon, young man." He briefly clasped Harland's shoulder before leaving the room and closing the door behind him.

Stella couldn't move. She had sat there frozen, watching the drama unfold in front of her, unable to feel or comprehended how much all of this affected her, not knowing how to respond. Harland stood nearby, watching her, apparently waiting for her to say *something*. All she could get to come out of her mouth was, "Mr. Ravensdale."

"The dubious Mr. Ravensdale, at best," he said. "When my real father died, this great man insisted on officially adopting me because he had no children of his own, and he loved me like a son. Harland Leatherby is the name I grew up with. He gave me his first and last name to go before and after it."

He handed her the document, and she unrolled it to look at the bottom, where he had just signed his name: *Benedict Harland Leatherby Ravensdale.*

"It's legal," he said, "but I don't know that I will ever feel worthy of the name."

Stella wanted to tell him he certainly was worthy of it. She wanted to tell him he had the heart of a raven. She wanted to tell him that some miracle had just occurred inside of her, where she had taken in the shock of this announcement, and rather than feeling angry or upset with him, she felt nothing but compassion and understanding, and she wanted all the best for him. She wanted to tell him she loved him and wanted to stay here with him and be his wife, but she feared that would sound too much like she only wanted to marry him so she *could* stay. Unable to find her voice at all, she could only stare at his signature and wonder how she would find the strength to stand up and walk out of the room to once again start her life anew.

"Read it," he said, jarring her back to the present.

"What?" she managed.

"Stop staring at my name and read the top. I didn't give it to you so you could look at it. I gave it to you because it's yours."

Stella frantically scanned the words in front of her and found herself heaving for breath as she realized she was holding the revised deed to Ravensdale, with all its land and properties.

"You can't do this!" she insisted, erupting to her feet with a sudden burst of energy.

"I can," he said, "and I just did."

"But this is not what your father wanted, Harland, and—"

"What he *wanted* was to know that Ravensdale was in good hands, and I have honored his wishes in the best possible way. He was not my father, Stella. As much as I loved him and he loved me, I do not have a bit of Ravensdale blood in me."

Stella dropped the document at her side and stepped toward him, putting her hand over his heart. "But you have the heart of a raven."

She saw the subtlest glimmer of tears brim in his eyes before he looked down at her hand over his heart, then back at her face. She wondered if he believed her, but knowing how he saw himself as a prodigal, perhaps it could take years for him to truly consider himself worthy of what he had been given.

In that moment, everything became perfectly clear to her. She knew what was right, for her and for him. And she knew it without any doubt, which made her all the more surprised when he stepped back and said, "I have to go, Stella."

"No," she insisted. "This is your home!"

"No," he said, "and let me make this very clear. I did not make this decision to trick you or to get you to feel sorry for me. My original plan was to remain here long enough to be certain Ravensdale was in good hands, and then I would find a life elsewhere. I didn't expect to fall in love with you. Now you know where I stand and what's important to me, but I can't stay here like this. I have more than enough money to live on, so you don't need to worry about me."

He started toward the door until she said, "Will you worry about me?"

He turned back. "Every day."

"Then stay," she said, her voice trembling.

"There is only *one* reason I could stay here in good conscience, Stella. Only one! And bear in mind that you are a terrible liar and you could never play poker."

Stella's emotion became difficult to contend with as she recognized his sincerity. He truly was determined to walk away with no expectations. And his integrity affirmed her feelings all the more. "Will you not stay because you love me?" she asked.

He gave her a sad smile. "No. You must understand, Stella, that staying only because I love you would be more painful for me in ways I could never put into words."

"Then stay because *I* love *you*. Stay because you know I'm telling the truth when I say that I knew days ago that marrying you was the only possible path my life could take if I truly wanted to be happy. Rich or poor, here or somewhere else, we have to be together." Tears fell down her face, and she said again, "Stay because I love you."

He smiled, and she saw his countenance relax. Had he been as afraid of leaving as she was of him going?

"Are you absolutely certain?" he asked, just as Mr. Meath had asked him just a short while ago.

"Absolutely," she said, just as she'd heard him say in reply.

"Well, then . . ." he said, holding out his hand.

Stella stepped forward and put her hand in his.

Harland kissed her, then looked into her eyes with conviction. "I think *this* is probably the best my father ever could have hoped for."

Count My Heart

by Sheryl C.S. Johnson

I reached over the armrest to steal some of Angie's popcorn. She looked at me and smiled tolerantly. I sank back into the soft theater chair, looking at the screen but not really watching the movie. I smiled contentedly and told myself I was happy not dating Jeff. It had only been two weeks since we'd broken up, and it was still difficult to make myself think of other things. Luckily, my roommate, Angie, was available to keep me busy. So far, I'd dragged her shopping and to the video store. This was our third movie. After having Jeff fill up so many of my hours, it felt weird to be alone. I hadn't realized how great Angie was until Jeff and I had broken up.

After the movie, as we headed out to the car, I admitted to her, "I'm going to miss you. Did you talk to your dad about keeping the apartment?"

Before she could answer, I had to cover my nose because of the sudden stench. I looked around for the source. An older, scruffy-looking man sat on the curb, leaning against the theater. He was watching us. We walked quickly out to the parking lot, where the air smelled less like urine and rotten fish.

Once we were standing between our cars, Angie said, "Yes, I talked to him *again* for you, and it's still a no. He's serious. In fact, he's already sold it, so it's a good thing we packed. Are you okay moving back with your parents for a while?"

I nodded, though I wasn't happy about the situation. I handed Angie my oversized soda while I dug through my purse for keys. The new impossible-to-style layers in my hair hung in my eyes, making me groan.

Angie laughed at me. "Trisha, you're such a dork. Your keys are in your pocket." I looked up at her, plunging my hand into my pocket, where I found my keys. She smiled condescendingly at me.

I hugged her. "I'm sure going to miss seeing you every day."

Her short brown hair lifted in the cold breeze. She opened the door to her black Civic and leaned against it. "Hey, it was fun, right? And I'll only be ten minutes away. You can come over when your dad drives you mad. My parents have a great couch downstairs."

I tried to tuck a tuft of hair behind my ear. This would be the last time I let Angie talk me into a new do. At least I hadn't given in to having it as short as hers. When we'd walked into the salon, she'd talked about blonde and playful. It was only through great efforts of obstinate glaring that I'd kept my natural rusty red. "Thanks for the offer," I said. "I'm sure we'll get along. My dad's been happier to see me since I don't live there anymore. He just about died of relief when I told him I wanted to move home again. Sure you're not going to sleep at home one last night?" I unlocked my car door, leaving my keys in the lock while we talked.

"On what? A blow-up mattress? No, thanks. But I'll be over tomorrow night to help you so we can load up my car too. I bet we're done by eight."

"Yeah." I shrugged. "Oh, shoot. I left my scarf." I started for the theater and called over my shoulder, "I'll see you tomorrow after work."

Angie called after me, "Good luck surviving that. Can't wait to hear about tomorrow's soap opera."

I stopped at the door to wave as she drove away. The scruffy man smiled up at me. When he opened his mouth, the smell intensified. I smiled back in the smallest way I could and escaped into the lobby before I took a breath. An usher was carrying my scarf out of theater 6 as I reached the doors. I thanked him and wrapped it around my neck.

I smacked my forehead when I got back to my car and saw my keys still hanging from the door. I yawned and blinked. It was the stress. Yes, I wasn't normally this stupid. I was just under a lot of stress with my new job . . . and the moving . . . and the breaking up. It was a lot to take on in two weeks. I slid into my seat, crinkling my nose at the breeze that carried the scent. I looked back at the building, but the man was gone. I rolled down the windows but couldn't stand the cold air very long. When I rolled them back up, the stench was stronger than ever. I pulled onto the road, glancing down at my coat to see if there was a spot the smelly man in the parking lot had touched. No, I would have felt that. I heard a small rustling sound inside the car. My eyes grew wide with alarm as I tightened my grip on the steering wheel and looked straight ahead, trying not to gag from the prominent smell I now realized was coming from *inside* my car. There was a gas station two blocks away. "Dang," I tried to say convincingly to no one in particular, "I need gas."

I pulled up to a pump, relieved to be under the bright fluorescent lights, and clutched my purse as I carefully pulled my keys out of the ignition. I slid out of the car, my heart beating in my ears and my eyes wide in the cold wind. A man wearing nice shoes and a thick tan sweater was pumping gas next to me. He pulled the nozzle out of his car and fastened the lid.

I stepped over to him. "Sir, could you help me?"

Just then a wild gust of wind pulled my hair in a dozen different directions. I sniffed the air but didn't smell anything. He looked at me warily. An image of what I must look like with my red hair splayed out in the wind flashed through my mind. I shook it off. He *was* handsome, but that was the least of my worries at the moment, though I couldn't help noticing how the wind didn't move his dark brown hair.

I nodded to my car. "Could you look in my car to see if there's an old man in my backseat?"

His expression changed. He looked around to see if anyone was watching before looking back at me like I was mentally challenged. "Sure," he said, slowly stepping past me to my car.

I watched him, not daring to look myself. He bent down to see past the glare reflecting off the window. He stood straight with a start. He looked at me, raising his dark eyebrows in surprise. "There is." He stepped to his pump and plucked the receipt from the machine. As he tucked it into his wallet, I shivered and rubbed at my eyes. He leaned over to me and, in a low voice, asked, "Is there supposed to be an old man in the back of your car?" He said it slowly, as though I didn't have the mental capacity to understand his question.

I glared at him. "No. I saw him at the theater, and then I smelled something, so I stopped here."

He inclined his head toward me, trying to understand. "You smelled something?"

I squeezed my eyes shut before opening them with a flustered sigh. "He was outside the theater, and he smelled bad. I had to go in and get my scarf. He must have climbed in my car while I was gone." I looked over my shoulder at the car and shuddered. "My car smells like he smells, so I stopped here just in case"—I shrugged—"in case he'd crawled into my car." I made the same face I used to make as a child when I saw a spider. I couldn't help it.

The stranger stood tall. "He looks like he's asleep." He nodded toward the gas station. "Why don't we go in and call the police. Just a second while I park my car."

I hadn't thought of calling the police and felt pretty stupid that he had first. I silently walked toward the store as he parked. Once we were inside, I felt cold. I couldn't help thinking that the guy could have grabbed me while I was driving or even when I got home. Thank goodness for poor hygiene, or I wouldn't have even known he was there. At the counter, the stranger I'd walked in with waited for me to say something but apparently judged from the spacey look on my face that I probably *was* mentally inept. He explained the situation to the store clerk, who called the police. I stood there staring vacantly out the window.

Near my ear, the man said, "Are you going to be okay?"

I came out of the trance and sucked in a deep breath. "Um, yeah. I'll be fine."

He thrust a hand toward me. "Nate Arden."

While he shook my hand firmly, I fought to spit out, "Trisha Pearson."

"Can I buy you a drink?" He motioned to the deli in the back of the store.

I looked outside, realizing I'd be waiting a while for the police to extract the smelly visitor from my car. I looked up at Nate. "Sure. Thank you." I couldn't exactly place the feeling I had when he spoke to me. His voice made my stomach do happy little flips, but it was tinged with a doctor's bedside manner. I shook my head. He was too young to be a doctor.

He ordered a lemonade for himself, a lime Coke for me, and some fries for us to share. We sat down at a little white table while we waited for the police and fries. I took a long sip of soda. "Thank you. This is really nice." I grimaced. "I didn't mean to bother you. I just wasn't really sure what to do."

"I guess what you do in a situation like that is pull into a gas station and get some help. You did the right thing." His eyes were light brown, and his lips curved the slightest bit at the edges, like they were waiting for a smile I thought would look natural there. He looked at me questioningly when I stared at him too long.

"You probably have places to be." I studied the gray flecks in the table.

"Actually, for the first time in a long time, I have nowhere to be. I was thinking about seeing a movie, but now I see what happens at the theater in a small town. I might rent one instead."

I smiled. "Logan isn't a small town."

"Oh, I see," he said unbelievingly. A clerk brought french fries, and Nate thanked him before grabbing one and sticking it in his mouth.

"It isn't a small town," I defended. "We have a college."

"You have a college. *It can't be small with a college*," he said, humoring me. He pushed the basket of fries toward me, so I took one.

"A *small* town," I explained, "has three or four houses and a little shack off the side of the road that says 'Post Office' on the front."

"I passed one of those on the way in. Are you sure that wasn't the Logan post office?" His face was placid as he studied me.

"That's Wellsville—a *small* town."

"Of course. So where is the nearest movie rental store in your booming metropolis?"

I laughed. "It's about three blocks south, but if you're not from here, they won't let you rent anything."

He leaned back and dabbed at his mouth with a napkin. The smile had appeared. Like a last puzzle piece, it made his face perfect. "I didn't think of that. Where's a Walmart? I'll have to buy a movie."

I took a long draw of soda. "Who says we'd have a Walmart? That's a pretty big store for a *small* town."

A shadow fell across our table, and we looked up at a policeman.

"Is that your green Sentra, miss?"

I perked up. "Yes. Did you find an old man in it?"

"Do you know a Lloyd Thompson?"

"No."

"I need to take down some information. We've put him in a more comfortable car. He was out cold."

I sighed in relief.

He motioned to Nate. "Are you the witness?"

"Yes, I suppose I am," Nate said.

"I need your information too." The officer sat down at the table and flipped through his notepad.

Nate looked at me, amused.

I suppressed a grin and looked away.

It didn't take long for the officer to take our statements. He handed me his card and a slip of paper with a case number before he left. The store was quiet except for the swishing sound of the clerk's broom down the aisles next to us.

I took one last draw of my soda and looked around the empty store before standing up. "Thank you for your help. I know it's ridiculous, but I was such a scatterbrain out there I'd probably still be standing there staring at my car if you hadn't been here."

"I'm sure you'd have made it in here on your own." The cashier at the deli made a show of turning off lights behind the counter, staring at us while he did it. Nate gathered the napkins and straw papers and tossed them into a nearby garbage. He nodded to the counter. "I think he's telling us he wants to go home now."

I rubbed a hand across my forehead and couldn't stifle a yawn. "I do too."

I gave Nate directions to the nearest Walmart as he walked me out to my car. He opened the car door for me and, before I could sit down, looked in the backseat and gave me a thumbs-up to say it was clear now.

Once I was behind the wheel, I jutted my hand toward him and said, "Thanks again for your help."

He took my hand and shook it. There was that smile. "Anytime," he said.

I glanced in my rearview mirror as I drove away. He stood under the bright lights, next to the gas pump, arms folded, watching me leave.

* * *

The next morning I pulled into the parking lot of Sandcorp and sighed, looking at the three-story building. The job I'd wanted for so long was just inside those doors, waiting to drag me down. I breathed deep as

I walked to the building, enjoying the freedom and the silence. It was only a short reprieve. After two weeks of working there, I knew the eye daggers everyone shot me each morning were waiting for me inside. It started each day at the head receptionist's desk. Her crusty look followed me until I turned a corner. That's where the file clerk usually stood up to glower at me as I climbed the stairs.

There was an elevator by the back entrance, but I kept telling myself I'd never use it. They'd all get over it eventually. *Eventually.* The problem was everyone had someone in mind for my job, but Mr. Pearson, the regional manager, had hired *me*. And as a *Pearson*, specifically one he'd fathered, I was doomed from the beginning. I didn't feel bad about it. Even if anyone could prove it was nepotism, I was the only one with an accounting degree to apply for the job. I wasn't going to lose sleep over it. What I *was* going to do was grind my teeth every morning as I applied my makeup and did my hair in gut-wrenching anticipation of the coming hours of work. I passed the file clerk. On time, as always, the properties management division stopped talking long enough to stare blankly at me as I walked by.

It was a relief to enter the payroll office, where the hostility was at least open and blatant. Nell looked up from her desk and rolled her dark eyes before looking back down to ignore me.

"Good morning," I said cheerfully. It was my goal to act as though I never noticed they all hated me. Nell, I learned from Trent, my only friend at work, had a sister in line to get my job. I pulled out my chair and draped my sweater over it. My desk was covered in neat piles of work. I looked through the glass behind my desk. Our office overlooked the main-floor work area. I sat down, and like every other day, I was sure I could feel people on the work floor staring up at the back of my head through the window. I hated that window. I forcefully stapled a stack of papers, smacked the stapler down on my desk, and stood up, heading for the bathroom. Nell followed me. "Hey, Barbie, did you get me those spreadsheets yet?" She followed me into the bathroom and stood too close to me, scowling.

"I put them on your desk." I faced the door and began peeling tape from the corners of the poster that hung there.

Nell squared her shoulders. "You can't do that."

I peeled a second piece of tape off. "Good to know."

Her glossy black curls touched my arm as she leaned in to put her hand over the poster. "It belongs here," she challenged me.

My stomach sank, but I couldn't stop there, or she'd always be in my face.

I peeled off a third piece of tape and glanced at the hygiene poster. "It's good to work with someone so health conscious." I peeled off the last piece of tape and carefully slid the poster from under her hand. I rolled it and marched back to my desk with her huffing behind me.

I unrolled it and began taping it to the window behind my desk. Wayne and Sarah joined Nell in front of my desk. Trent wandered in, his sport coat draped over one arm and his briefcase in the other hand. "Score one for clean hands!" His attempt to lighten the mood failed as usual.

I smiled appreciatively at him and sat down to do my work. Wayne, Sarah, and Nell stood at my desk for another minute before returning to their own. We all listened to Nell call my father to tell him there was a problem he needed to see. I pretended not to notice, sending a file to the copier to print. I was retrieving my copies when my father walked in.

His hair was as red as mine, setting off his tired, blue eyes. "What now, Nell?"

Nell didn't look up. She just pointed to the window with her pen.

I looked nervously at my dad, who was searching my face for an explanation. On the poster, a cartoon of Spanky the Hand dancing with a bar of soap reminded us to wash our hands. I shrugged innocently.

He ran his fingers through his hair. "I'm not seeing the problem here."

Nell smacked her pen down on her desk and stood up. "You're not seeing the problem? How can you *not* see the problem?" Trent inched to the door to close it before we could draw too much attention. "She has moved company property without permission. That"—she pointed her long finger at the poster—"belongs in the women's lavatory."

I stood behind my father. "It's obviously been there a few years. I think they've memorized the concept of washing their hands by now," I said.

"That's not the point!" Nell hissed.

My father looked at me. "Patricia," he said in his most formal tone, "why have you relocated the poster from the women's bathroom?"

I shrugged. "I'd like a little privacy. Do you have any cubicle walls?"

The edge of my father's mouth twitched as he tried not to laugh. "All the cubicles are in use." He looked quickly at Nell. "At any rate, you don't have enough seniority to warrant a cubical. There's a waiting list."

I nodded. "Can I borrow the poster?"

He took my elbow. "Can I talk to you in private a moment?" We stepped into the hall, and Nell looked triumphant as I closed the door behind me. "Unless you have a real affinity for *Spanky the Hand*, I'm going to have to ask you to put it back where it belongs. This is tough enough. You don't need to rile them on purpose."

I exhaled a defeated breath. "I hate seeing them stare at me. It's bad enough when it's in my own office, but the whole work floor can see me." He looked at me blankly. "Dad, they all hate me." I wanted to explain to him that this was just one more thing in a rotten month. There was the breaking up with Jeff that had me melancholy. I hoped Jeff was happy with that Carman girl he said he'd felt a connection with. And even if my father was glad to have me home, I had been happy living with Angie. It was going to be so hard to be home with Mom and him. I had been queen of my own space for a blissful year, and now I'd lost that.

Feeling sorrier for myself by the moment, I scanned my life for more pity fodder. The bum in my car last night had to be one of the scariest things that had ever happened to me. But thinking of the bum in my car reminded me of Nate Arden, and I couldn't help smiling when I thought of him standing there, staring after me as I drove away. He was one handsome knight in shining armor.

Bringing me out of my thoughts, my father said, "It's out of my hands. I can send them a memo, but that's about it. Show them what you're made of, and they'll come along." It was the fourth time he'd told me that.

Trent opened the door, sticking his head out. "Sir, if it was a different poster?"

My father beamed at him. "Sounds good to me." He turned and headed back to his office.

Trent squeezed into the hallway, closing the door behind him. "My little girl has a box full of Disney posters she can't stand."

"Really? Ask if we can use them. I hate everyone staring at me like that."

"It will pass."

I shook my head. "My dad says that."

"You're just the new kid with a bad rap. It will improve. Nell isn't nice on her best days. I heard Sarah and Wayne laughing about the poster. Another two weeks and you'll be out of the woods."

I studied the floor. "This isn't at all like I thought it would be. I should quit so they can hire someone else."

"Listen, whoever they would hire wouldn't make everyone happy because everybody was rooting for someone different. It might as well be you. I saw the applications. Like I told you, you were the most qualified."

"Thanks, Trent."

"C'mon, don't sweat it. Let's go tell Nell Mr. Pearson said *she* can put the poster back now."

I laughed.

* * *

After a long day at work and a few hours of moving, Angie and I collapsed onto my parents' couch. I wiped a dusty hand across my forehead. "I think that's it."

"And in two hours." Angie stretched, reaching out to give me a high five. "Who needs men?"

My dad walked by, whistling with his car keys still dangling from his hand.

"Dad, are you just now getting home?" I called out.

He stuck his head into the room. "Hello, Angela. Working late today makes a good tomorrow." He disappeared down the hall.

I shook my head at Angie. "That reasoning is so flawed on so many levels I don't even know where to start."

Angie sat up, wiping her hands on her jeans. "Did you tell him about the guy in your car?"

"He's got so much to worry about. No reason to feed his anxieties. Besides, nothing happened."

"What about the big-city guy? Will you see him again?"

"He's from Cleveland. It's not like it's New York—and no."

"Cleveland is big. And you're a dope. You should have asked for his number."

"Because after having some weirdo creep into my car, I should top it off by hitting on a complete stranger."

"He bought you a Coke."

"You're right. I really enjoyed that Coke." I thought of Nate's handsome face. "I'm a dope."

* * *

I pushed a sheet of cookies into the oven. My mother came in carrying a stack of dish towels. "Thank you for helping. You're a lifesaver," she said as she tucked them into a drawer.

"No problem." It was part of living in the Pearson house. I was the free babysitter, the part-time maid, the resident doctor, and any number of other responsibilities that came with being the oldest child. My little sister Mikelle needed to bring cookies to a school activity in the morning, and even though I was exhausted from hefting heavy boxes and wasn't even finished unpacking, I stood dead on my feet whipping up a batch of chocolate chip cookies.

I pulled the beater from Mikelle's hand before she licked it. "We still need that. Let's be sanitary." I would have thought that would be obvious to a twelve-year-old.

"Can I have some dough, then?" A strand of her long hair stuck in her mouth.

I sighed and pulled a spoon out of the drawer and loaded it up before handing it to her.

"I'm glad you're home. You make the best cookies," she said.

The doorbell rang. I grabbed a cookie from the cooling rack and jogged down the hall. I knew everyone would be waiting for someone else to get it. When I opened the door, Nate Arden was standing there in a Herringbone sport coat and a blue striped tie. I stared at him, surprised.

He blinked and asked, "Does Kent Pearson live here?"

I nodded and mutely held the cookie out to him.

He took it, not smiling and looking puzzled.

I motioned for him to sit down in the sitting room. Heading down the hall, I reviewed my fuzzy pink slipper socks, my raggy blue sweatshirt, and my crazy hair clipped up in five different places. I poked my head into the laundry room, where my parents were folding clothes together. "Dad, some Arden guy is out here for you."

My dad suddenly looked cross. He smacked a hand on the dryer. "The nerve of corporate never ceases to amaze me. They gave me five assignments. He thinks I can't handle that?" My father stood up, tossing a pair of folded socks onto the pile of laundry. "Morning isn't soon enough to get nosing around in my business?" His grumblings echoed after him when he left, and I exchanged a concerned look with my mother. I glanced down the hall, thinking of returning to talk to Nate but deciding not to. I climbed the stairs slowly, catching the first of their conversation. "*Mr. Arden*, what can I do for you today?" My father's voice was controlled but edgy. It's how he'd talk to me before we learned how to make peace. I felt sorry for Nate but told myself he was lucky. It was much worse when it was your own father staring you down like that. What was I thinking? Nate was from corporate. He was probably worse than my father. My ears perked when I heard Nate's voice.

"I'm going to need these files first thing in the morning. Could you have them waiting for me?" My mother passed the staircase and looked at me over the top of her glasses. I was obviously poised to eavesdrop. I smiled sadly and disappeared to my room, where I unpacked distractedly as the sound of my father's raised voice vibrated through the floor. I guessed my father was letting Nate know what he thought of getting a visit at home. A few minutes later, I stood at my window and watched Nate leave. He looked up at me from the sidewalk. I didn't drop the curtain. There was no use pretending I wasn't watching him. He stared for a moment longer before he turned and strode purposefully to his shiny black rental car. Whatever my father said to him, it didn't look like it had upset him at all.

I bounded down the stairs two at a time and found my father in the sitting room, leafing through a binder, looking more cross than ever. "Dad?" He looked up. I bit my lip, building up courage. "Who is Mr. Arden?"

"He's a man I'm going to have to work with for a while."

"What does he do?"

My father took off his glasses and folded them. "He's from corporate. I'm not exactly sure what he does." He pointed his glasses at me. "But we're going to watch him like a hawk. I can't think of a time corporate has come sniffing around that turned out better than before they got here."

"So he's a sniffer?"

"I'm not sure what he is, besides trouble."

* * *

I hitched a ride with my father in the morning. Why should we both drive? He pulled in beside Nate's shiny black rental. Nate was waiting inside the foyer, drinking something from a Styrofoam cup. He looked like an ad for men's clothing. In fact, he looked so polished it would have been a shame to touch him in case it left a wrinkle. I thought of his tan sweater and shiny shoes the first night I met him. I bet he thought he had dressed down. Looking at his flawlessly polished shoes, I found myself wondering if his socks were pressed as well.

On the way up the main staircase, my father looked like he was carrying the weight of the world on his shoulders. I knew it was Nate's fault. Nate followed like a shadow behind us. My father hadn't even acknowledged him. I didn't see the use of watching Nate like a hawk if we didn't have to.

My father looked murderous when I paused so Nate could catch up to me. As we walked up the stairs side by side, I asked, "Mr. Arden, what exactly do you do at corporate?"

He finished his drink and straightened his tie. Without looking directly at me, he answered, "I'm an accountant." My father let out a snort ahead of us.

"Why did they send you here?" I asked.

He looked at the back of my father's head meaningfully and answered, "To account."

My father looked back to give me a sarcastic *nice going* look.

I shrugged.

In the payroll office, I found my desk covered in rolled posters. I was the first one in the office, so I pulled off the rubber bands and opened the posters. Some were sports cars covered with bikini-clad, busty women.

Others were movie posters. When I opened my e-mail, I discovered one from Trent asking for poster donations the day before. "Wow." I glanced at the clock. I still had ten minutes before everyone else arrived. Here was my shot at privacy. I grabbed my scotch-tape dispenser and went to work.

Nell was the first to arrive. She blinked, her always-tired face looking unimpressed. "Nice car."

"I think it's a Porsche. I bet Wayne will like this one."

Nell shook her head. "I don't want to look at that all day."

I stood back from the window. "I guess I don't either. Why don't we say whatever goes, but anyone has the right to cover anything."

Nell sauntered over to my desk and started looking through the posters. She looked up. "I think we have enough to do the whole window." I raised my eyebrows in disbelief when she said, "C'mon, let's roll up our sleeves before anyone tells us we can't do this." She opened one and started laughing. "I'm facing this one out."

I'd never seen her smile before. She proudly held up a picture of two monkeys yelling at each other with the caption, "Quit monkeying around and get back to work."

Thirty minutes later, Wayne taped the last corner of the last poster. The room smelled like permanent markers because Sarah had greatly edited the woman on the Porsche to the point that she had a new mustache and sunglasses.

Trent shoved his hands deep in his pockets. "That is a work of beauty. The 'Got Milk?' one is my favorite. Sorry it isn't Disney. My kid was more attached to those than I thought she'd be."

Wayne grabbed a ball cap off the filing cabinet and covered his heart. "I think we should have a moment of silence for our fishbowl. May it rest in peace and never return."

We gave a unanimous amen. Unfortunately, my father and Nate walked in at that moment. I was the only one with the sense to look guilty because I was the only one who realized corporate was in the room.

My father was stunned into silence. Trent stepped forward. "You said any other—"

My father waved him off. "This is Mr. Arden. He needs full access to all of our files. Nell, you know them best. You can help him with whatever he needs."

A smug smile crept across my father's face. In the corner of the room was an old desk nobody wanted, with peeling laminate popping off the edges. It was piled two feet high with old files. "There's your desk." He clapped Nate on the shoulder and turned to leave.

Nell put her hands on her hips, glaring at Nate. "And *why* do you need to see our files?" Her words were laced with attitude. I would have felt bad for Nate, but it was nice having Nell aim it all at someone else after two weeks.

"I have a little auditing to—" Nate began.

"*Auditing.*" Nell nodded. "You dance in here in your fancy getup and expect us to bow down and kiss your feet. Tell me you're not from corporate."

Wayne looked him up and down. "Oh, this smacks of corporate."

"He's corporate." I smiled kindly. Nate's eyes barely flickered to me, but he communicated more in that one look than he had over a basket of fries. I pursed my lips tight so I wouldn't say anything else.

Nell snaked her finger toward him. "Last time corporate waltzed in here, all of us got a 10 percent pay cut. You can find your own files, Mr. Arden." Nell pulled out her chair and daintily sat down, dismissing his existence.

Everyone silently returned to their desks. I began to back away as Nate studied his desk for a moment. "Trisha, can I talk to you in the hall for a minute?"

Everyone's heads whiplashed my way. I walked to the hall, keeping my eyes down.

In the hall, I folded my arms and looked him in the eyes. "What can I do for you, *Mr. Arden?*"

"*Mr. Arden* now, is it?"

"You couldn't know this, but until this morning, I was everyone's number-one person to hate here. I've just been bumped to number two." I smiled. "If I call you Nate, we might be in competition for number one again."

"Is that right?" He studied my face for a moment. "As a representative of corporate, I have access to . . ." He stopped, looking thoughtfully above my head as he continued. "I have the power to appropriate certain company assets while I'm here to help me do my job."

"What do you need?"

"In the world of business, there are tangible and intangible assets. Tangible assets would be in the category of things you can—"

"I know what tangible assets are, Mr. Arden."

"And some assets are intangible, meaning you can't touch—"

"Surprisingly, I also know the meaning of intangible."

He continued like I hadn't interrupted him. "Them. This would be things like knowledge or, in a way, staff."

"Could you get to the point? I'm sure they're getting crooks in their backs trying to listen to this conversation through the door."

Nate looked at the door. "*You're* going to be an appropriated asset."

"I'm not an asset. A chair is an asset. A computer is an asset. I am a person."

"I said intangible."

I pointed down the hall. "Could you excuse me for a few minutes?"

I rushed to my father's office, slipped inside, and shut the door, leaning against it. My father leaned back, his jaw slightly clenched. He exhaled and said, "That bad already? This is just the beginning."

"Could *I* be considered an intangible asset?" I asked.

My father laced his fingers thoughtfully. "An argument could be made for that."

"Can he appropriate assets?"

"Oh, that's clever. Right to my daughter."

"Dad, can he?" I couldn't keep the panic from my voice.

My father studied his glass desktop. "I think it's best if we generally avoid the topic of work until this kid hikes back to Cleveland."

"Can he?" I almost shouted.

My dad nodded.

"Everyone already hates me. This isn't helping."

He shrugged. "Take it up with the boss. Sorry, kiddo. This one's over my head."

I took my time returning to my office. Nate was sitting behind my desk, watching Wayne lift file boxes off the desk in the corner. My mouth dropped open.

Nate rolled his eyes. "I'm not taking your desk. Wayne's just helping me out. I've been explaining the concept of appropriated assets to everyone. You'll be happy to know they've volunteered you as being very helpful." I looked at Trent, whose eyes darted to Nell.

Nell was glaring at Nate, surely thinking of where he could shove his appropriation powers. I looked around the room. "It's true. I just checked with Mr. Pearson. There's nothing we can do about it."

Nate stood, offering me my chair. "As I was saying, I'll cause you as little inconvenience as possible. I have, however, been sent here to do a job, and I'm going to do it."

While Nate set up his computer and ripped some curling laminate off his desk, I finished my most important work first, just in case he didn't leave me any time later. I appreciated the complexity of the work because it kept me from worrying about corporate and what they were planning for our branch.

When it was time for lunch, everyone left promptly, except Nate. I stood up, gathering my sweater and purse. He was leaning over his laptop, adjusting wires. He'd shed his sport coat and rolled up his sleeves. I studied his short, dark hair, the way it swooped to a peak in the front and feathered down at the sides. His sideburns crept down a little, giving way to the smooth olive skin of his cheek.

He looked up at me. "What?"

I blinked, shaking sense into my head. "Do you want to go to lunch?"

He sat down on the edge of his desk. "Is that, *Do you want to go to lunch, Mr. Arden?* or *Nate, would you like to grab a bite to eat?*"

I suppressed a smile. "It's not your fault you're corporate."

"It is too. I worked very hard for it to be exactly my fault. But I'm not the enemy."

"Mr. Nathan Arden, do you want to go to lunch or don't you?"

"Nathaniel."

"No kidding? Mr. Nathaniel . . ."

"I prefer Nate."

I groaned.

He laughed. "No. I've got a lot of work to do. Thanks for asking though."

I headed for the door. "Hey, asset." He pulled out his wallet. "I will, however, need to eat." He handed me a twenty.

"What do you want?"

He shrugged. "Surprise me."

I sat down at my desk and pulled out a pad of paper. "Do you like spicy food? Have any allergies?"

He raised his eyebrows and looked at me reproachfully. "Surprise me."

"Okay, but don't whine to me when you don't like it."

I was almost out the door when he said, "Get yourself the same thing and hurry so we can eat before they get back."

I rolled my eyes at the impossibility of that.

It did turn out to be possible though, since his presence inspired everyone to take a full lunch elsewhere. He insisted that I pull my chair to his desk so we could eat together. I handed him his change.

"You see," he explained, "if I have you get the same thing for yourself, I know you won't get me anything horrible." He took a bite of his sandwich. "This is pretty good."

"I wouldn't get you anything horrible."

We ate in silence. Afterward, I gathered the wrappers and wiped his desk with a napkin. "Hmm," I said. "I bet your desk at corporate is a little nicer than this one."

He nodded. "It is, but only marginally. I have a pretty big cubical."

I smiled, sitting on the edge of his desk. "I pictured you in your own office."

"Corporate doesn't mean better. It just means somewhere else with more work."

"And more power," I added.

He laughed and looked at the ceiling. "This is the first time they've given me power, and so far, to be perfectly honest, it kind of stinks."

The way he said it was decidedly sloppier than anything else he'd said to me, making me wonder if he was partially human behind the perfection.

"Nell knows a lot more about files here than I do. Why am I the asset instead of her?"

He shrugged. "I like you the most. I can pull any of them anytime though, but why?" He pointed at me. "That isn't corporate talking. It was off the record."

"I think I can tell off the record when I hear it."

"Just crossing my *T*s."

An hour later, he placed a list of files he needed on my desk. I knew where to find most of them. Unfortunately, that meant spending quality time with the file clerk who shot eye daggers at me every morning. Deciding I wouldn't get far with the clerk on my own, I walked over to Nate's desk and leaned down to talk to him. He was creating an elaborate spreadsheet on his computer.

"Can you come with me for a minute?" I whispered. "I need you to do that intimidating corporate czar thing you do."

He stood, unrolling his sleeves. Everyone watched as he followed me out of the room, shrugging into his suit coat. He didn't ask questions in the hall.

As we approached the file desk, I told him over my shoulder, "This won't take long. I just need to flash you around for admittance. If I were drowning, these people wouldn't save me."

We stopped in front of the desk. "Because of your father?" he asked at full volume. The clerk looked up at us.

"Because Mr. Pearson is my father, yes."

I put his list in front of the clerk. "Mr. Arden from corporate will be needing these files."

Nate looked suddenly interested. "As soon as you can, please," he said in an authoritative tone.

The clerk took the list and hustled to open cabinets. I looked up at Nate. "Thanks. That was all I needed."

He looked around at the vast expanse of cubicles. "So now I just leave you down here with the wolves?"

"I'll be fine," I assured him.

He turned and started to walk away. Then he turned back, coming to stand beside me. "I'll wait with you."

"Then two of us aren't working."

"Ah, but the files come faster if I stand here. When I have the files, I can really start working."

"What are you looking for?"

"Discrepancies."

"What kind?"

"I can only tell you what I told your father."

I leaned forward. "What was that?"

"He didn't tell you?"

I shook my head no.

"Then it isn't my place to say, but whatever it is, you can help me find it."

"That's great. Just great. I should be *super* useful with all of that forthright and enlightening knowledge under my belt."

"You will be." He smiled, looking forward.

By the end of the workday, Nate's desk was surrounded with boxes of files. The steady click of his keyboard filled the room. The normal office banter was absent. As though they'd been watching a conductor, Nell, Trent, Wayne, and Sarah stood up at precisely five o'clock and silently filed out the door without a good-bye. I slowly gathered my things. When I stood, Nate looked up, though the clicking of his keyboard continued. "I need you to get this list of reports from your father. I'll need them first thing in the morning."

I took the list from him. "It's five now. Time to go."

He looked at his keyboard. "Good-bye, Miss Pearson."

I nodded. Studying my shoes, I said, "It's Miss Pearson now, is it?"

He smiled up at me, his face brilliant and beautiful. If my father knew Nate could do that, would he like him more? I wondered. Nate focused on his typing again. "Good night, Trisha."

"Good night, Nate."

* * *

Three weeks flew by while I worked with Nate. He didn't leave me enough time to notice if anyone glared. If I wasn't finding files, I was setting up appointments or typing receipts into his complicated spreadsheet while he read them off. There were thousands of receipts—never-ending boxes with files of receipts. Each receipt had a corresponding entry already existing in the computer. He was checking to make sure the hardcopy matched the soft copy. On occasion, he'd find a discrepancy of pennies and color code it and store the offending receipt in a box by his desk. He never did tell me specifically what he was looking for. As each day passed, he grew more frustrated at not finding it.

And with each passing day, I forgot more and more about my breakup with Jeff. I didn't have to try to keep myself busy at home because I was usually staring into the distance thinking about the way Nate smelled when he leaned down to my desk to tell me what to enter in his spreadsheets, thinking about his habit of giving his desk a triumphant rap when he thought he'd found something, thinking about the way he'd smirk at me whenever Nell complained about anything. I loved that smirk, the one he showed only to me.

One morning I bumped into Trent in the break room as he was pulling his brown-bagged lunch out of the fridge. "Long time no see."

"I guess I've been pretty busy." I shrugged.

"After three weeks of doing your job, I'm sad to say it's the most boring thing I've ever had to do." He sat down at a table, and I sat beside him. "Was it boring to you?" he asked.

"I never got to do it long enough to get bored. It wasn't exactly interesting. This assistant-to-a-crazed-corporate-accountant gig isn't bad though."

"I thought you'd be hating it."

"What's to hate? He barely talks, except to himself, and my whole job description could be summed up with the words *go fetch*. No one's glaring at me anymore."

Trent took a bite of his sandwich and, with a full mouth, said, "I told you it would blow over."

"Maybe, or maybe they're too afraid to glare with Nate hovering."

Trent's eyebrows raised. "Nate?"

"Um, Mr. Arden."

"Did *Mr. Arden* ask you to call him Nate?"

"No. Not at all . . . I just . . ." I fell silent.

Trent looked like he had nowhere else to go and all the time in the world to wait for an explanation that would satisfy him. "Yes . . . *you just?*"

"I met him at a gas station before he came to work here."

"He worked at a gas station?" Trent chortled.

"No. He was getting gas. I needed some help. I didn't know who he was, and he didn't know who I was. We haven't even talked about it. It's just when I met him there, he told me his name was Nate, so I have a hard time saying Mr. Arden instead."

"What kind of *help* did he render?"

"This is a really stupid story. Are you sure you don't have some pressing question about my job we could go over instead?"

Again, he looked at me, blinking, as though he had all the time in the world.

I sat down at the nearest table. "You're going to laugh."

Trent shook his head in denial, sitting down beside me.

"Okay, I was at the movie with my friend, and an old man hid in my car. It smelled funny, and I could hear him in the backseat, so I pulled into the nearest gas station and got out. Nate stayed with me until the police came, and that's that. Nothing."

"Sounds like an adventure to me."

I pointed at him. "And no one else wants to hear it. Promise me."

"I promise. If you made that up, you stink at making up stories. You could've done better."

"Thanks, but it's true, and somewhere there's a cop or two who can back my story." I looked sideways to avoid Trent. "Or Mr. Arden could." I put my hand on Trent's arm in an awkward gesture. "But do me a favor, and don't ask him."

"I wouldn't deign to bore him with a story like that."

"Thanks, Trent."

* * *

That night I stealthily shuffled down the dark hall in my slipper socks. My teenage sister, Steph, jumped out at me, shocking my arm. The blue arc of electricity stood out in the darkness. "Shoot!" I rubbed my arm. They were all faster than me. I guess sitting at a desk all day was making me soft. I held my hands in the air. "Okay, I give. All done zapping."

Mikelle stood up from behind the recliner, only visible as a silhouette. "Ohhh, why?"

"Because I'm losing, and I'm sure if one more electrical current runs through my body, my heart'll stop beating. You can zap each other as much as you want. *I'm* off-limits."

Mikelle turned to Steph and reached out to shock her shoulder. Soon, everyone was screeching. The house sounded like an elephant stampede. I pulled off my socks and dodged a shrieking pair of children. I barely heard the doorbell and had to stop to consider if I'd heard it at all. It chimed again.

I ran down the hall and opened the door. Nate was standing in the dusk, still dressed in his formal pinstriped suit from hours ago. I had to laugh. "You poor thing. You've really got to get a life. Come on in." I ushered him into the sitting room.

When I turned on the light, a chorus of "Turn it off!" roared down the hall.

I turned it off. "I hope you don't mind sitting in the dark for a minute."

"It's fine." He sat down on the very edge of the couch. "Is your dad home?"

"If my dad was home, we'd have the lights on." A triumphant shout echoed from the family room. "And it would be quiet."

I could see him smile but only faintly. I looked up at the dark ceiling, sad that I'd missed the full effect of the smile. I turned on the light and shouted, "Movie time. Seth, pop the popcorn." I turned to Nate. "Just a sec. I'll get the monkeys settled and be right back. Make yourself comfortable."

As quickly as I could, I played eenie meenie miny moe to see who would choose the movie. Seth was walking in with the popcorn as I pushed play. "Remember, I'm the one who gets in trouble if you spill the popcorn, so it will be *me* who makes you pay. I need toilets scrubbed, so spill away. Wah ha ha ha!"

I bounded down the hallway, back to Nate. I sat down on the piano bench, facing him. "So, working late?"

"It's what I do."

We stared at each other. I spent my time memorizing the tip of his nose, its perfect angle. He probably spent his time wondering if I always paraded about with fuzzy pink socks poking out of my pocket.

He perched closer to the edge of the couch. "How much influence do you have with your dad?"

"Not much. He's a really good man. He gets along with all of his children, except one." I looked down at my feet, wishing I hadn't let Steph paint my toenails bright blue.

"I need your help."

"I'm the *one* he doesn't get along with, so whatever you're going to ask is an exercise in futility. We have spent the last three years cultivating a perfect relationship where we say as little as possible to each other yet hug often. It's a balance we're proud of."

"He needs your help."

"You can ask, but I'm not making any promises."

"Someone has been embezzling from your branch." He paused as I gasped. "Corporate is looking to make some cuts. I was able to call them off, but if I can't find the information I need, they're ready to shut down the whole branch."

"They can't do that!"

"They're itching to cut costs in this economy. Let's face it, there's nothing you do here that can't be done in a dozen different branches."

I stood up. "That's over two hundred jobs." Nell would think nothing of that 10-percent pay cut after this.

"Two hundred twenty-one jobs. I've been counting. I need some reports from your father, but he's taking his time. He doesn't understand how serious this is. I know corporate hasn't cultivated the best relationship with their branch managers, but they still pull the strings."

He put his palm out as though it was a piece of paper, and he drew on it with his finger. "See, these reports will show the branch is profitable." He looked up. "And it is. It's got one of the highest profit margins. I need these reports because it will help me pinpoint what part of the region the money is leaking from. Historically, the western region performs the same way every year. It didn't last year. I can't spend a month cataloging receipts. Corporate is calling every day, and every day, I don't have anything to give them. It's the lead I need to get out of his hair and call off the dogs. If he really wants me gone, he's got to start helping me."

I heard the kitchen door open, car keys dropping to the counter. "I'll try."

"Trisha." My mother's voice echoed down the hallway.

"I'm in here with Mr. Arden."

My father appeared around the corner. He stood straighter and squared his shoulders when he saw Nate. "Patricia, could you excuse us?"

I silently ducked out of the room and headed to the kitchen to help my mother put away groceries. We worked silently as we strained to hear their conversation. It was difficult until my father started raising his voice. I cringed, calling to mind Nate's smile, hoping Nate would keep a calm head when my father couldn't.

"I'm not hiding anything. I've let you crawl all over that office! You can tell corporate . . ."

"I'm not insinuating you're hiding anything! I've been through your records. I know it isn't you. Not getting me what I need is the same as protecting whoever is doing it. You understand that, don't you?" Nate's voice was hard and commanding. I realized I didn't know him as well as I thought I did when I couldn't imagine what his face would look like when he was using that voice.

At this point, I could only imagine my father's heroic attempt to keep his mouth shut. His arms would be folded tightly across his chest, his eyes set in defiance. At least his mouth wouldn't be open.

"I'll expect them on my desk tomorrow morning," Nate said.

The next sound was the front door opening and closing.

When I began to leave the kitchen, my mother caught me by the hand, shaking her head no. I squeezed her hand, giving her a reassuring smile as I continued to walk out. In the sitting room, I perched where Nate had been. My father was standing with his fists jammed into his pockets, and he was staring silently out the window. "Dad," I said in my smallest voice, "do you know corporate wants to make cuts and that they're thinking of shutting us down if they can't get to the bottom of this soon?"

He looked at me, his lips thin and tight. He scratched at something on his forehead. I waited for his reprimand. His voice was quiet too. "The worst part is that it's happening on my watch," he said. "I should have seen it first, not some pencil pusher at corporate. I knew the numbers were low. I was sure we'd pulled the profit, but there it was, suddenly red. It never occurred to me someone was dipping in." He sat down heavily. "Do you know how many people have access to do something like this? How many ways they could be doing it? If he shuts us down . . ."

"Mr. Arden isn't going to shut us down, Dad. He's going to keep us open. We just need to help him do it." I shrugged. "He's not corporate. He's just an accountant. He needs help."

My father didn't say anything else. He left the room. I listened to the scrape of car keys on the counter, the small *pip* sound of him kissing my mother good-bye, and the kitchen door opening and closing.

I was nearly done with the dishes, and my mother was singing the last lullaby when he came home. I dried my hands as he flipped a manila envelope onto the counter. "Mr. Arden's at the Quinton, room 206. Don't suppose you'd be willing to . . ."

"Tonight?"

"The sooner the better."

I looked down at my wet blouse. "I'm going to change real quick."

It didn't occur to me until I was halfway to the Quinton that I now looked more dressed up than I had when Nate had seen me earlier. I hoped he wouldn't think I'd dressed up for him. Thankfully, my hair had started working in my favor, and instead of cursing Angie silently each morning, I thanked her for the change. The blue shirt I'd chosen was trimmed in lace and, according to Jeff, made my eyes prettier than the heavens. I sighed, realizing that thinking of Jeff didn't make me feel wistful or even sad.

I told myself I didn't care if Nate liked the way I looked as I walked down the hall of the Quinton. I rapped on door 206. No one answered. I knocked again, then considered pushing the envelope under the door. I bit my lip. Whatever was in there was pretty important. What if I had the wrong room? I had just turned to leave when I heard the latch. Nate opened the door, wearing a white robe. His hair was wet, sticking out at odd angles like it had just been towel dried. I couldn't help the greedy grin that spread across my face. I had caught him not being perfect. Except . . . I tilted my head sideways to study him. He looked really handsome. My expression fell. He made messy hair look good. It was like going to the mall and seeing a gaudy outfit that would look good only in a third-world country, then seeing it in the tabloids on the rich-and-famous-looking très chic.

He opened the door wide, inviting me in. "Just a minute." He stepped into the steamy bathroom and shut the door. I sat down at a little table and studied his temporary home. It was a sad little room. No wonder he worked late every night.

He came out, catching me snooping in the travel brochures and restaurant receipts on the table. I looked up guiltily. I held up a brochure on hot-air ballooning. "Just snooping where I probably shouldn't be."

He took the pamphlet from me and tucked it neatly back in a pile. I handed him the envelope, hoping it would make him forget my snooping.

His hair was imperfectly finger brushed, and he was wearing an olive-green T-shirt and blue jeans. It looked unnatural to me after seeing him in business attire for weeks on end. I looked down at his bare feet, feeling like an interloper just because I could see them, while he studied the contents of the envelope. He smacked the papers with the back of his hand and laughed. "I should have asked you for help four days ago. How did you get this?"

"I reasoned with him. He's really not that bad. He just doesn't . . ."

"Like corporate. They need to work on their HR relationships. Sometimes I don't like them, and I work there. Maybe if they made more contact that wasn't disciplinary."

I stood up to go, and he motioned to me. "Um . . ." He looked around the room. "Uh, don't go. Let me get you a soda." He scrambled to open a tiny fridge and tossed me a Sprite. "We should celebrate."

I looked down at the can in my hand. "Hurray," I said blandly.

"You don't understand all the work this saves me. It's just what I need to get corporate off my back."

I couldn't help looking sad when I thought about him leaving sooner.

He took the can from me, popped the lid, and handed it back. He clinked his can to mine. "To persuasive blue eyes." He raised his eyebrows.

I smiled uncertainly before taking a sip. We stared at each other for a few seconds before I started for the door again. He beat me to the doorknob. "Call me pent up and starved for company, but would you like to go to dinner?"

"Nate, I ate dinner three hours ago, like normal people do."

"Okay." He shrugged. "Do you want to go with me while I get dinner and you stare longingly at my food until I give in and give you half?"

I laughed. "I don't know."

"Oh, good."

"Good? How is that good?"

He pulled a pair of socks from a drawer and sat down at a little table, where he started putting them on. "Because if you don't know, I can make up your mind for you, and I say we go. I'm starved."

"I have to be back by ten. I work early."

"We'll get take-out."

* * *

At ten after ten, I crept past the kitchen. I stopped when I heard my father clear his throat. "That took a long time."

I turned to look at him. "Not really."

"Where have you been?"

"Out."

"Out with Mr. Arden? How interested is this man in you?"

"I don't know," I answered honestly.

"You wouldn't complicate already-complicated situations by dating him, would you?"

He wasn't asking me; he was telling me. "No, of course not."

* * *

Looking at Nate in the morning made it hard to believe I'd ever seen him the night before. His hair was styled stiffly into perfect place. There wasn't a hint of stubble on his face. He wore a shirt and tie and burgundy sweater vest under a dark-blue sport coat. I looked at my watch, giving him forty-five minutes until he was too hot and had to take off the sport coat.

When he eventually pulled off his sport coat, I looked at my watch. He had lasted twenty minutes longer than I thought he would. He filled my first few hours by having me find different kinds of files. When I entered the office with my arms full, he was looking through Trent's drawers. Trent had pushed back from his desk and was waiting good-naturedly. Nate took a box of checks back to his desk, flipping through them and recording something.

He returned the checks to Trent before recording Wayne's and Sarah's. He didn't get a chance to fish through Nell's desk. She handed him her checks without looking up from her ten key. As had become the habit since Nate occupied the office, everyone stood at noon to take lunch. I stayed with Nate. As soon as the door closed behind Trent, Nate jutted his chin toward me. "Look in your checks and tell me you're missing 316, 327, and 364."

I pulled out my box of checks. "I'm missing 316 . . . 327 . . . and 364. How did you know that?"

"I'm good at my job. I found the leak, and it's from your desk."

"But I didn't . . ."

"No, you didn't, unless you started sneaking in before you were hired, which would be hard without security clearance."

"How did you figure it out?"

"The reports your father gave me helped me identify unusual spending per state." He reached out to draw on the desk with his index finger. "Every state is profitable, some less than usual, but Montana is down by 50 percent . . . Then you go through and look at expenditures, and the receipts add up." I was trying to look like I was keeping up, but I must have failed. "Three checks to George Rush were cashed. We don't employ a George Rush. I found the beginning of the trail. Everyone else has the wrong numbers. It had to be your desk by process of elimination."

He stood up, pacing excitedly. "There are a lot of Montana expense receipts that are off five dollars here and five dollars there. Over the year, it's added up to be substantial. Fifty cases of printer ink were purchased from the Montana account. We don't have that type of printer anywhere, and I have yet to find the ink."

I turned to look out the window behind my desk, peeling down a corner of a poster to see out. I looked down on the bookkeepers. "Who has access to my checkbook?"

"As I see it, Trent, Sarah, Wayne, and Nell."

I shook my head, still studying the bookkeepers. "I don't think it was them."

"I can't say for certain, but I don't think it's them either." Nate gathered a few papers, placing them in a neat pile. "Didn't I see some microwave popcorn in the break room?"

"Yeah, for a buck twenty-five a bag. Who would pay that?"

Nate reached for his wallet. "The schmuck from corporate. We're going to watch some movies." He handed me a notebook, a dollar, and a quarter.

"Grab a pen and your sweater. The basement is cold."

Nate and I made our way across the work floor with the aromatic bag of popcorn. Luckily, most people were still at lunch. A few heads popped up from cubicles but went right back down when they saw Nate. He looked past them, zeroing in on Leroy Hunt, who was driving a forklift loaded with boxes of paper near the loading doors.

Leroy jumped down from the seat when he saw Nate coming. Nate held a hand out to him. "Leroy, I'm Nate Arden. I hear you're in charge of some of our security here."

Leroy nodded cautiously.

"I need to review a few security tapes. If I give you some dates, can you get me the right footage?"

"Well, I don't know." He lifted his ball cap and ran a hand over his smooth scalp. "I can get you a range. There's more than one week per DVD. And the recorder only runs at night."

"Whatever you have, I'd love to see it."

I looked behind us. A few curious eyes looked around their cubicles. I followed Leroy and Nate through a steel door and down some stairs. We arrived in a large broom closet, where a small television sat on a little metal desk. Nate sat down on the only chair. Leroy stretched to reach around him to a little black box with a white switch. "Here's the current feed. 'Course we're not recording now. No need to with so many eyes." He pulled out a box. "What you have here are the discs of old feed. The date range is written on the label." He pointed to the little television. A few employees were standing, staring in the direction of the steel door we'd just entered. I could see where my desk should have been behind the blank side of the posters. "This here is the date and time it's recorded." Little white digits flashed in the lower left corner of the screen.

"Thanks, Leroy." Nate shook his hand again. Leroy left but returned a moment later with an empty paint bucket he turned upside down for me to sit on. I smiled appreciatively at him and sat beside Nate, handing him the popcorn. He handed it back. "That's for you. I'm watching my weight."

I blew a piece of hair away from my eyes. "Did I mention how embarrassing it was to carry this smelly popcorn behind you all the way across the floor? Everyone was looking."

Nate was flipping through discs. "You care too much what other people think."

"Is that so?"

"Mmm-hmm." He pulled out a disc in a red case.

"And you're watching your weight?" I asked, incredulous.

"I don't want to get buttery fingerprints on my papers," he said.

"Oh." The man was quirky. He turned to me and opened his mouth so I could drop a piece of popcorn in. He crunched down on it and smiled, leaving me dismayed when I realized I could happily shovel popcorn into his mouth all day.

An hour later, we found the first date we were looking for. We watched the dimly lit work floor for thirty minutes before we found the fast forward function on the player. "Stop!" I yelled when I saw a flash of white on the work floor. Nate rewound the video, and we leaned toward the little television. I squinted as my eyes followed the white jacket. "I think that's Sarah."

She climbed the stairs and entered the office. I could barely see my desk. Sarah set something on her desk and sat down. A moment later, a dark figure moved across the workroom floor. It was a man with brown hair. I couldn't see his face. He headed up the stairs. I could barely see him as he entered the payroll office. Sarah stood quickly as though she was startled. Then he lunged at her. I gasped, horrified to be watching the attack. Another minute of viewing, though, made it evident that she was *very* happy to see him. I leaned back and looked away. "I'm not sure we should be watching this."

"Look." Nate was holding his pencil to the screen when I looked. Both people were gone.

"Where did they go?"

"I think they're on the floor. They dropped right here." He smiled at me. "By your desk."

"Ew."

"It was four months ago. It wasn't your desk yet." A few more minutes passed with them out of sight on the floor.

"This is the worst movie anyone has ever taken me to," I said.

Nate looked at me. "Can't expect too much from movies in a small town." He winked at me and looked back at the screen. I doodled on the notepad Nate had me bring until he asked, "Do you know this guy?" He paused a frame.

I squinted to see him but couldn't make his face on the tiny TV. I shrugged. "I'm embarrassed to say I don't really look at people here. Besides, I've only been here a few months. Nell knows everyone."

He took the bag of popcorn from me. "Go get Nell, then."

I stood up. "Okay, but she isn't going to be happy."

"Tell her the truth."

"Original approach. I have your permission to tell her anything I know?"

"Anything that has to do with work."

"Be back in a few minutes."

When I got back to the office, Nell was hanging up the phone. She looked at me. "Like they wouldn't know you need to file a 2041 before asking for the advance. Who doesn't know that? I swear someone feeds these people questions just to tick me off. Some big *tick off Nell* list is floating out there, and they're reading right from it today."

"I've got something for you to look at. Could you take a break for a few minutes?" Sarah, Wayne, and Trent all looked up.

Nell narrowed her eyes. "'Cause I don't have work to do?" she asked sarcastically.

"I'm sure you have work to do. Mr. Arden just needs you to look at something." Trent stopped typing, and the room was silent.

Nell stood up. I swiped her jacket from the back of her chair. "You'll need this."

"I'll show him appropriated asset." She grabbed her jacket out of my hands and started walking. "*Get me this. Get me that!* 'Yes sir, your Dry Cleaned Highness. Can I spit polish your shoes, sir?'" The door closed behind us.

"He's not that bad," I told her on our way down the hall. She was quiet. Before we reached the work floor, I turned to her. "He's trying to help us. Corporate wants to shut us down because someone's taking money. Mr. Arden is fighting to show we're profitable, and he's going to find the person who's taking the money."

Nell stopped. "Run that by me again."

"Someone is embezzling money. Mr. Arden needs to find them so he can save the branch. With the money gone, it looks like we're not profitable, and corporate is looking for ways to cut back. They'll take down the whole branch."

Nell was staring at me. She barged ahead of me, storming through the workroom. "Well then, let's find the—"

"The crook," I said before she could finish her sentence with a string of colorful words. "You mean the crook, not Mr. Arden, right?" I whispered as loud as I could without anyone we passed hearing.

Nell stopped. "For someone with a degree, you sure aren't that bright."

I sighed and opened the steel door leading to the broom closet downstairs.

When we got to the room, she stood in the doorway, blocking me. "You tell me what you want, and I'll make it happen," she told Nate.

Nate looked at me, raising his eyebrows in surprise. "What did you say to her?"

I shrugged. "The truth."

"Let's get this thing done." Nell sat down on my bucket.

Nate tapped the screen with his pen. "Do you know who's with Sarah here?"

Nell squinted. "He looks familiar, but I don't know his name."

Nate pushed back in his chair, exhaling in frustration.

Nell pursed her lips. "I don't know why you're messing around with this podunk TV. I can get a better image off my laptop. I've got some video-editing software."

"Really?" Nate's face brightened. "You good at that kind of thing?"

"Sure am." Nell let her head tilt back to look behind her and command me, "Go get my laptop from under my desk, then I need you to finish my Idaho entries."

Nate looked at me expectantly. I groaned inwardly as I climbed the stairs. Now I was Nell's asset.

"So Nell's in trouble, huh?" Trent asked me when I returned to the payroll office.

"Something like that," I mumbled as I fished around under her desk for the laptop bag. I slapped it triumphantly on her chair.

Sarah's eyes were wide. "What did she do?"

"I'm not privy to that kind of information. I just do what I'm told."

I steamed as I walked back to the stairwell. I tried to shake it off. Having Nell boss me around wasn't half as bad as Nate's expectant look.

I opened the steel door. Nate was waiting at the top of the stairs. He took the laptop from me. "No one can know what we're doing here. If we tip off the thieves, they'll be harder to catch."

I looked at him blandly. "They think Nell's in trouble for something. I'm letting them think that."

Nate nodded. "Good. Have fun with those Idaho entries."

"Sure. Lots of fun."

As I worked, I told myself it didn't matter that Nell had bossed me around. Work was work whether I was working with Nate or entering numbers. It was all part of an eight-hour day. I looked frequently behind the desk at the postered window, wishing I could see the steel door. With Nate gone, the room was full of Trent and Wayne's happy banter, with an occasional quip from Sarah. I'd forgotten how that sounded. At five, they stretched, yawned, and pushed away from their desks to gather their things.

Trent stood at Nell's desk, waiting. "You coming? Time to go home."

"Um . . . yeah." Five o'clock. I grabbed my purse, sweater, and coat. Downstairs, I couldn't help staring at the steel door.

I waited for my father in the parking lot. After five minutes, I went back inside to find him. He was still in his office on the phone, laughing. I sat across from him, yawning.

He hung up the phone. "Usually, I'm waiting for you. Isn't *Prince Uncharming* keeping you late?"

"Not today."

"What exactly took you so long last night?"

"I watched him eat his dinner." I sat straight and leveled my eyes at my father, daring him to say anything else.

He did the same. A practiced silence hung thick between us, tense and familiar.

A rap on the door made me look up. Nate walked in and pointed at me. "You didn't even say good-bye. I need to talk to your dad for a few minutes, then I'll tell you what we found."

I waited on the couch outside my father's office for ten minutes. When they came out, neither one looked happy. My father held his briefcase and coat as he headed down the stairs.

"I'll meet you at the car," I called out after him.

He didn't respond.

Nate stared after him silently.

I picked up my sweater and purse. "It's nice to know there's someone in the world who can upset my father more than I can."

He looked at me like he'd just woken up. "Oh . . ." He blinked tightly before focusing. "I found the guy. Rather, Nell identified him.

He stays. In the video, he stays after Sarah leaves, and he's clearly rifling through your desk. He's the supply clerk. We've got him on three other tapes, same scenario."

I nodded and started walking to the door, afraid to keep my father waiting. "Great."

Nate kept pace beside me. "We have to keep it silent. I'm working with a detective from the police department now. We're going to see if we can catch the guy this week. He meets Sarah on the same day every two weeks." He put his hand on my arm to stop me before I opened the door. "Thank you for all your help."

He was looking at me funny. I cocked my head to the side, thinking. In a panic I asked, "Are you leaving?"

"In an hour or so."

"To go back to Cleveland?"

His face dawned understanding. "Back to the hotel." He smiled. "You don't want me to go." He looked happy about it.

I studied the floor. "I was just curious if you were leaving." My father honked the horn. I turned and looked anxiously out the glass door.

Nate put his hand on my shoulder, turning me to him. The horn honked again. I took a step toward the door. Nate rushed the words. "I have to work on the floor, and you'll stay at your desk this week. It needs to look like I'm on the wrong trail, or this guy will get wise and bolt. The detective says it's the nail in the coffin if we catch him while he's doing it. Either way, we have a case, but this way it will prosecute smoother."

My face fell, thinking about not being with Nate every day. "That makes sense."

I put my hand on the door bar and pushed. The cold air blew in. Nate put his hand on the bar next to mine. "You should get gas tonight around seven. You wouldn't want to run out."

I looked at him quizzically. He propped the door open farther for me. I slipped outside into the cold wind. When I sat down in the car, my father didn't wait for me to put on my seat belt.

As we pulled onto the main road, he turned on the radio. "You don't so much as look at that boy this week, you understand? We can't have you messing this up."

I leaned my head back and stared out the window. "I'm not going to mess anything up." I realized that my father probably thought I was dating Nate. I looked at him, wondering if it was his idea to put Nate on the floor for the rest of the week. It didn't matter. I studied the weave in my sweater. It *was* a good idea because at least he wasn't going back to Cleveland. I smiled. Nate had noticed that I didn't want him to leave, and he didn't look unhappy about that at all.

At 6:50 that night, I shut the door to the dishwasher, dried my hands, and pushed the start button. I poked my head into the den, where my father was reading. "I'm going to gas up my car. Do you want anything while I'm out?"

He glanced up at me. "No, thanks."

Down the hall, I found my mother reading to Mikelle. "I'm going to gas up my car. Do you need anything while I'm out?" She flashed a smile at me, shaking her head.

As I pushed the key into the ignition, I couldn't help feeling that it was too easy to sneak out of the house. I used to have to work harder at it when I was a teenager. I pulled up to the gas station and pumped gas into my car, staring at Nate's car. When I was done, I parked next to the building. He was waiting at a table in the deli with a basket of fries and two drinks.

He looked up, smiling. "I would have ordered more for you, but nothing looked good." He was still dressed in his work clothes.

"I wasn't expecting anything, so this is great." I sat down across from him. "To what do I owe the honor of dining on fries and"—I took a sip of my drink—"lime Coke? You remembered?" I smiled warmly at him.

He smiled back and leaned forward. "I spent a lot of time with Nell today and a lot of time without you. I deserve this."

"Really? So it's an issue of entitlement?" I said teasingly.

He laughed. "It's an issue of greed. I'm happier when you're less than ten feet away." He picked up a fry and popped it in his mouth. I did the same, mulling over his words and hoping they meant what I thought they did. He wiped his hand on a napkin. "Your dad is good at getting what he wants. I don't think he likes me."

"It's not that he doesn't like you . . ."

"No. It *is* that he doesn't like me. He's grateful for everything I'm doing. He practically gushes with gratitude. Since you've talked to him, he's bending over backward to help me, and the farther away he arranges to have me from you, the more help I'm getting. I get a cubical tomorrow."

"It makes sense to have you farther away from where the thief will strike, so it doesn't all have to do with me."

"He has let me know in plain, blunt terms that it unequivocally does."

"What did he say?"

His brow wrinkled as he studied his drink. It was the same look he got at work when he tweaked his spreadsheets. He wiped a hand across his face. "It doesn't matter. I'm not going to get between your father and you."

"It matters to me."

"Trisha, you get one family, one shot. You don't mess with that."

I pushed my chair back from the table. "Thank you for enabling my father to live my life for me. He loves that." I started to stand.

"Don't." He tugged on my sleeve.

I sat down. He pushed my drink toward me. "How do you feel about driving yourself to work tomorrow and bringing some casual clothes?" He reached into his pocket and pulled out a folded piece of paper. He put it in my hand. "You could meet me there at five thirty."

"Why?" The address didn't look familiar.

"Just wanted to talk."

"I could probably do that."

He pulled out a few dollar bills. "I need to get going." He grinned. "It's date night."

"You have a date?" I couldn't help my frown. That made him grin bigger. He held the gas station door for me, and we stepped out into the cold.

"*Sarah* has a date," he said. "The detective is meeting me there." He stood by my car. "Trisha, I don't want to make your life more complicated." He reached out a hand to brush away a lock of my hair, and he stepped closer. "I don't want to be an issue between you and your father." He slid a hand into my hair behind my head and pulled me to him. "But I don't think I have a choice because I have to do this."

"Have to catch a crook?" I asked. I'd never been that close to him before. His eyes warmed me, and I felt weak in the knees, wishing so badly that he'd kiss me. I lifted my hand to his arm and smoothed my thumb over the herringbone texture of his sport coat, never taking my eyes from his.

His grin twitched up on one side as he lowered his lips to mine. "Have to catch *you*." My knees felt weak as his warm kiss drove away the chill. His kissed me once, then twice, and stopped only after the third kiss. His eyes held mine as he pulled away. "That was about what I thought it would be."

I put a trembling hand to my chest, wishing he hadn't pulled away. "Sudden?" I asked.

"Worth it," he replied.

He opened my car door for me. I slid into the driver's seat, and he shut the door. By the time I reached home, I'd relived those kisses a dozen times.

* * *

The next morning, I stood in the break room next to Nate, staring at a vending machine. He held two quarters, sliding them against each other. I knew everyone was staring at us. I could feel the tingle on the back of my head. "Nate," I glanced quickly up at him, "how was your date?"

He shrugged, "Satisfying . . . both of them." He winked at me before he plunked his coins into the machine and punched a button. He took his prize and walked out of the break room, me staring after him and everyone watching me do it.

I turned back to the machine, deposited my money, and punched the button a little too hard. "Just ask him if he's leaving," I muttered to no one in particular as I made my way up the stairs, not caring how hard I jostled my soda. He couldn't leave now. It couldn't just be over. Sarah wasn't at work, and Nell had been flashing me knowing glances all morning. Once I was in the payroll office, I spun my chair around, looking down at the work floor cubical I knew held Nate's desk. The posters were rolled neatly beside my desk. Nate had posted an official declaration from corporate that unsanctioned posters weren't allowed. We'd had to take them down the day before, and we'd all paused for a moment of silence before we did it. I was the only one who knew it was so the surveillance camera would have a view to my desk. After this whole mess with the embezzlement, I was betting I'd never again see a time when the cameras didn't have a clear view to the payroll office.

Trent had returned my job to me first thing that morning, only now it was organized and much easier than it had been. Before the day was through, I'd finished all of my work. What had been taking me two days took less than one now. Nell was back at her desk. I rolled my chair over to her. "Do you need any help today?"

She looked up from her ten key and blinked slowly. "What?"

I shrugged. "I'm out of work, and I have more than an hour to burn before we get off. Can I help you with any of your stuff?"

She sat up straight. "You're *out of work*?"

"And obviously you're not, so I can help." I forced cheer into my voice.

She pulled a drawer open and smacked a thick file onto my lap. "I need these employees to receive this letter." The letter fluttered lightly, landing on the file. "That ought to keep you going for at least an hour." She opened another drawer and pushed a box of blank envelopes toward me.

I took them, smiling with gratitude. "Thanks, Nell. I hate feeling useless."

She hunched over her ten key again. "Saves me from feeding envelopes to the dragon. I hate that thing." Nell was the only one who referred to the copier as the dragon. She was also the only one who had trouble with the envelopes. Of course, I pondered as I awkwardly scooted my chair back to my desk, she was the only one who printed envelopes.

At ten after five, my phone rang, startling me and making me bump my head on the copier door. I'd been wrestling jammed envelopes out of it for fifteen minutes. I wiped my forehead with my arm, careful not to get toner on my face with my blackened hands. I pulled a tissue from the box on Nell's desk to protect the phone as I answered it. "Trisha Pearson here."

"Oh no. You see," Nate was laughing, clearly visible as I looked down at him, "Trisha Pearson needs to be somewhere else. She's in the wrong place. She's got a date in twenty minutes, and she's not even dressed for it." He pulled his tie off and draped it neatly over his cubical wall.

"I'm getting dirty. I need to unjam the copier before I can wash up and change my clothes."

"You get going. I'll clean up the jam. I'll be right behind you."

"Wait. No. You can't come up here. I wouldn't want to scare a thief off."

"All taken care of." He walked into the office, flipped his cell phone closed, and shrugged out of his sport coat. "Don't take too long."

My father was sitting at his desk reading a book when I walked into his office to say good-bye. He bent down the corner of a page before setting the book down. I stood, waiting. He pursed his lips before asking incredulously, "Where are you off to?"

"I have a date . . . with Nate."

He stroked his chin. "So it's Nate now? What happened to *Mr. Arden*?"

"I guess he was never really *Mr. Arden* to me." He stacked some envelopes in a tidy pile on his desk and started putting away pens and paper clips. He didn't look as mad as I'd expected him to. "You're not upset?" I sat down across from him. My brow wrinkled as I thought of half a dozen things to say and what trouble they might create between us.

"Leave it to you to go running to the one thing I tell you to stay away from. I'm not upset. You were right. Nate isn't corporate. He's a man. You're an adult, and it's none of my business. Besides, you could do worse than an accountant from corporate."

I studied his bright blue eyes. Finally, I smiled, reaching across the desk to take his hand. "Dad, I love you."

He stroked his thumb across my fingers and smiled, picking his book up. He squeezed my hand and let go. He sighed and said again, "None of my business." When I stood up to go, he added, "I love you too."

I smiled back at him before shutting the door.

Nate was outside leaning against his car and tossing his keys. He called to me. "That took forever."

I glanced at my car and realized I didn't need to hide that I was going on a date with Nate. I walked to him. "How about we save on gas and you drive?"

He nodded toward the building. "Your father . . ."

I caught his keys midtoss. "My father is fine with it."

On the way, Nate told me about Sarah's date. "The police had your whole office wired so they caught everything. Sarah had a discussion with her boyfriend after their usual tryst . . ."

"Oh, yuck. They got the . . . They got it on tape?"

Nate chuckled. "Oh yeah . . . But as I was saying, they had a discussion, and it turns out that Sarah was in on it too. It was her idea. Apparently, she didn't know about the security cameras. We have enough evidence now to send them away for a long time."

"That's why she didn't come to work?"

"She was still locked up this morning."

Nate pulled into the parking lot of a little Mexican restaurant. "I hear the food here is great."

I looked dubiously at the fluorescent-green, rotating cactus out front. "Who told you that?"

"Trent."

"Oh, okay, then." Nate took my hand and led me into the building. While we waited to be seated he kept his arm possessively around my waist.

Over burritos and fajitas, we laughed about the tense weeks at work. I sat back, absently stirring my ice cubes with a straw. "I thought I really wanted this job, but it hasn't turned out to be anything like I wanted."

"They like you now . . . or at least they will when they discover what you've helped me find."

"It's not about being liked. I thought it was, but it isn't. Not now."

He stood up and moved over to my side of the booth. "Then what is it?"

I had to turn to look up into his face. "You were the best part of work, and now you'll be gone."

He leaned down and kissed me. With half-hooded eyes, he said, "I asked you here to tell you about a job in Cleveland."

"You're not going to be an accountant anymore?"

"Oh, I am. I'm getting my own office at corporate. They told me today. However, from my office, I'll be able to see the properties division . . . and an empty cubical that old Stanley Stennor used to sit in until he retired last month. They're still taking applications . . ."

I leaned over and kissed him hard. Between my kisses, he mumbled, "'Course, it's just a bunch of paper pushing." I reached my arms around his neck and hugged him tightly. Out of breath, he said, "Did you know company policy allows dating outside of your division?" He laughed. "But I can see you're not interested, so you probably wouldn't want to know anything about the relocation package they're offering with it." He kissed my ear and my neck.

I pulled back and smiled at him. "Oh, no. I'm not interested at all." I leaned forward, smirking. "How soon before I can move?"

* * *

Three months later

Nate walked into the properties division carrying a long cardboard tube. He tossed it onto my desk, and it rolled over the papers I was inspecting. "What's this?" I opened one end and slid out a rolled poster. It was from Nell. On the top corner of the battered Spanky the Hand poster, she'd left a Post-it note that said, "Congrats on your new job. Love, the gang." I laughed hard, wondering if I shouldn't just hang it in the bathroom for old time's sake.

"I passed the mail cart on the way here. Sheila asked me to bring it to you. This is so far out of the way," Nate said.

I sighed. "I know, but the view is to die for."

Nate looked around. "What view? When it gets dark like this, I can see the city lights, the skyline. My new office is awesome at night. Which reminds me, why are you working so late?"

I huffed. "Carlton wanted all Midwest properties alphabetized, copied, and the copies filed by account number . . . before Tuesday. I figure if I work four hours overtime for three days, I should have it done on time."

"That's some impressive dedication for a cubical without a view."

I laughed. "Oh, my view *is* better than yours." I stood up. "You can't see it too good in the dark, but in the day"—I pointed to his office window—"I can see this hot accountant sitting in his office." I put my arms around his neck. "And you can't beat that." He kissed me and held me around the waist with one arm as he pulled out a little black gadget that looked like a flash drive from his suit coat. He clicked the gadget and motioned to his office.

"That office?" he asked.

His office window lit up with red Christmas rope lights that spelled out "Trisha, marry me."

I stepped back from him, slack-jawed. "Where did you get Christmas lights in June?"

He swung me toward him and kissed me, half laughing. "*Christmas lights in June?* Are you going to marry me or not?"

"Well, your condo is bigger than my apartment," I quipped. He looked wounded. I kissed him softly. "And I do love you more than I love breathing. I'd marry you in a heartbeat."

He kissed me and, without moving his mouth away from mine, managed to say, "Trisha, I don't want that poster in our house." I giggled and reached over to my desk so I could toss the poster into the trash.

OTHER BOOKS BY SHERYL C.S. JOHNSON

Table for Two